Reflect - Text copyright © Emmy Ellis 2023
Cover Art by Emmy Ellis @ studioenp.com © 2023

All Rights Reserved

Reflect is a work of fiction. All characters, places, and events are from the author's imagination. Any resemblance to persons, living or dead, events or places is purely coincidental.

The author respectfully recognises the use of any and all trademarks.

With the exception of quotes used in reviews, this book may not be reproduced or used in whole or in part by any means existing without written permission from the author.

Warning: The unauthorised reproduction or distribution of this copyrighted work is illegal. No part of this book may be scanned, uploaded, or distributed via the Internet or any other means, electronic or print, without the author's written permission.

REFLECT

Emmy Ellis

Chapter One

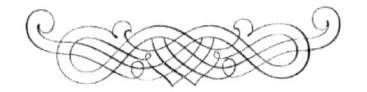

At the wake, Nessa mingled with the mourners in the pub she ran for The Brothers, the Noodle and Tiger. Although 'mourners' was the wrong term. No one seemed particularly bothered that her father, Dickie Feathers, had died. Too much laughter going on, too many smiles. Too many people here for the free booze and food. *She* didn't even care that he was dead. She'd welcomed it, ensured his murder had happened. When her mother sold the house and moved away, Nessa's life would be even better.

Even more so once she'd dealt with Dickie's lover, Miss Marlborough, except Nessa wouldn't be killing anyone like the woman had asked. Plus, she had a half-brother to meet. Chesney, eighteen and trying to be like his ex-gangster dad, a man who'd been employed by Ron Cardigan, sent into retirement by the twins when they'd taken over the estate. Chesney, a lad who'd panicked and royally fucked up, meaning his mother had come to Nessa at the crematorium earlier and asked for help.

Nessa had to be careful, though. She worked for the twins, and they'd get arsey about her walking into the lioness' den tomorrow without telling them first. Worse, they could think she was going behind their backs and take the pub away from her. She should phone them now, tell them what was going on, but something inside told her to see things for herself before she went scuttling to them. Marlborough's story could be a load of old bollocks, the woman manipulating

Nessa's feelings for whatever reason. Maybe to hurt Nessa's mum?

Today was the first time she'd met Marlborough properly, so she had no reason to take her words as gospel. Marlborough and Chesney ran a drug business for Dickie—news to Nessa until a couple of hours ago—and apparently, an addicted pregnant woman had turned up for some gear. Things had gone wrong. A premature baby had been found at the church recently, but Marlborough could have been lying when she'd said Chesney had pushed the mother and set off the labour. She could be lying that the mother was now chained up and held against her will.

Marlborough wanted Nessa to kill her, like Dickie would have done.

All Nessa wanted to do was free her.

It was odd to have what amounted to a stepmother who was eight years older than her. Dickie—Nessa didn't want to think of him as Dad anymore—had gone for someone twenty years his junior. Mum had always claimed he'd been having an affair, but Nessa hadn't believed her. The thing was, Mum was prone to whispered tales that were all bullshit, and Dickie had quickly shut them down. Like he'd shut her spirit down. Nessa's, too, until she'd grown a backbone and struck out on her own, making a success of the pub. Before that, she'd been a barmaid in various boozers, not a manager, and while she was tough and could be gobby, all she'd wanted was to be recognised in her own right, not as Dickie's daughter. Now, she wanted to be recognised for doing the right thing, and if there *was* a woman held in Marlborough's office, she *had* to get her out of there.

Nessa's sixty-something mum came by, dabbing at her cheeks with a scrunched tissue, pretending she was the grieving widow. Mum was just as happy as Nessa that Dickie was dead, but she played the part well.

"When can we leave?" Mum whispered. "Making out I give a shit is killing me."

Nessa had been shocked the other day at Mum's revelation. She'd been meek and mild for years, taking whatever Dickie had dished out, but that had been an act, too. As soon as news had come in of Dickie being dead, her true colours had seeped through, and Nessa's hatred of her had increased so much it was suffocating. All those years when Mum could have shown a stiffened spine, standing up for her daughter, yet she hadn't. Dickie had bullied Nessa her whole life, and the one other person who should have stepped in and stopped it had sat idly by and let him get on with it.

Is that a good enough reason to ask the twins to kill Mum, too?

Dickie hadn't been in that coffin. The fish in the Thames had eaten him long before the cremation, bricks put in the casket in place of his body. The twins had persuaded a man at the crematorium to help them cover up the death, although Nessa didn't want to know how.

She dragged herself back from her thoughts to answer the question. "We haven't been here long enough to go."

"Yet another hour or so he doesn't deserve from me." Mum sipped her G&T, no husband around to tell her to rein her drinking in anymore.

"Think of this as the last day you have to do anything regarding him. Tomorrow is the start of your new life." *And mine.* "I'm not enjoying this either, you know, not that you'd care of I am or not."

Mum narrowed her eyes. "I never did like you much."

"I know."

These types of comments no longer hurt, thank goodness. Numbness had set in a while ago. Nessa had learned to like and love herself, something she hadn't thought possible. The twins' faith in her had helped, which was why she felt guilty about keeping this Marlborough shit from them. Still, better that she saw things for herself than send them in, all guns blazing, only for them to find an empty office with no chained-up woman in sight, Nessa looking a prized plum.

Mum swanned off to speak to Karen, one of Jordy's ex-wives. Jordy, Dickie's best friend, wasn't here, nor were any of the others in that geriatric gang. The story was that Dickie had died in a car accident, his face too wrecked for Mum to identify him, and as for the rest of the gang, people believed they'd done a heist and fucked off with the proceeds. In reality, George had killed them for their attempt to raid their gun-and-drugs stash hidden in their recent acquisition, a hairdressing salon called Under the Dryer, but some didn't buy the tale.

Not that George and Greg cared.

Nessa wandered to the buffet table. She'd asked the chef to go old-school, with cheese and pineapple on sticks, all the kind of food her father and his cronies would have had in their youth. It was nostalgic, because Nessa remembered past parties, where the DJ went from the sixties through to modern day, all the ancients getting up to jive around to 'Wild Thing' by The Troggs but tutting at anything by Adam Ant or Pearl Jam. Music played now, 'Stand by Your Man', Tammy Wynette, and Nessa snorted at the irony. Mum had certainly done that, right until the end.

Stupid cow. They could have had a much better life on their own. Then again, Nessa doubted Mum would have loved her more if it had been just the two of them. Maybe the hate would have been worse because Nessa was a constant reminder of Mum's attachment to Dickie. Maybe Mum would have left her with Dickie, God forbid, and swanned off for a better life alone.

Nessa loaded her plate with triangle sandwiches filled with beef paste, a few crisps, and a butterfly cupcake. She turned to survey the crowd. Ed Parsons, one of Dickie's mates who hadn't been in the gang, swayed to the music, arms held high, shouting the lyrics and earning himself a swift elbow in the side from someone who didn't appreciate his gob. Others sat and chatted, necking drinks back, and many stood around gassing as if this was someone's birthday party, a reason to celebrate.

How many other people were happy Dickie was gone? Loads, Nessa reckoned.

Someone came in, a young bloke with floppy blond hair. His black suit and tie pegged him as a mourner, and even if she hadn't known he existed, she'd still have thought he looked like Dickie. Chesney must have thought it was a good idea to turn up, but it wasn't. He was the last person Mum would want here. She'd have a shit fit if she saw him. Nessa's initial instinct was to get her mother out of here before she clocked him, but that instinct belonged in her past. She no longer had to sort things out for her parents anymore, and besides, she'd told herself she'd blacken her father's name now he was dead, and this was a perfect way for it to happen. It wasn't like she cared how Mum felt, was it?

Let it play out.

She positioned herself at the end of the buffet table and leaned against the wall, her food taking the place of the proverbial film-watcher's popcorn. Chesney glanced around, perhaps for a familiar face—who knew whether Dickie had introduced him to anyone here. These people would have willingly kept that bastard's secret. Chesney marched up to the bar, arrogant confidence in every step, and Nessa immediately disliked him. He was Dickie all over again. Drink handed over by Susie, Nessa's shift manager, he took it towards Mum, his intent clear. Without his father there to stop him, he was about to either introduce himself or give her his condolences.

What he didn't realise was that Mum had seen him before and knew who he was. Sparks were going to fly now Mum had rediscovered herself. Nessa almost blurted out a loud laugh. She stuffed a sandwich in her mouth.

Chesney stood beside Mum who gave him a quick glance, frowned, then resumed her conversation with Karen. It seemed her brain had caught up, reminding her who he was, because she turned to him, eyes wide, cheeks flushed, and threw her G&T in his face. Chesney idly blinked away the droplets from his eyelashes, not fazed one bit.

Fucking hell!

Nessa ate a crisp.

"Get out!" Mum said, easily heard over the music. "Get out and never come back."

"I wasn't aware you ran this pub, Mrs Feathers." Chesney sounded posh, possibly an affected accent. "I can come here if I want to. The place hasn't been closed to regular customers, has it?" He gazed around, a Dickie smirk in place.

"You're not welcome here, not today," Mum said.

"What, I can't come and raise a toast for my dearly departed old man?"

Several gasps went round, and a couple of "Oh, fuck me!" popped out. Those who'd clearly known about Chesney watched avidly, smiling, while those who didn't appeared confused.

"Your old man?" Mum screeched, louder than she'd spoken for years. "Old man? Got a DNA result to show me, have you?"

Chesney took a hankie out of his suit pocket and casually wiped his cheeks, patted the drink droplets on his expensive jacket. He pointed to his face. "Does it look like I need one?"

Mum couldn't deny Chesney's parentage if she tried. She'd been with Dickie since he was young, and the similarity at the same age was startling. "Fuck off out of here, you piece of scum."

Chesney laughed, a toff's titter. "I rather think *you're* the scummy one here. You've always been common, Mrs Feathers, whereas my mother and I—"

"I don't want to hear *fuck all* about your slag of a mother," Mum belted out, years of keeping her mouth shut unleashed. "Cheap, she is. Can only snag someone else's husband, can't get one of her own. Living off the money my husband made, never doing a day's work in her life. Delusions of grandeur, that's her. I wouldn't be surprised if she's got the clap she's slept with that many men. I've seen her, flirting her arse off down the market."

Nessa choked on her second crisp. Who the hell flirted at the market? Mum had seen what she'd wanted to. Nessa coughed to clear her throat, drawing attention to her.

Mum swung her gaze to the buffet table. "Are you just going to stand there and let him talk to me like that, Nessa?"

Tell her, go on. Stand up for yourself. You owe her jack shit. Think of all the years she didn't care about you. "Why not? It's the same as you did when Dickie shouted at me."

A few people clapped. A flustered Karen tried to guide her friend away, but Mum was spitting angry now she had a voice.

"Get off me, woman," she snarled and pushed Chesney's chest.

He held firm, chuckling at her ineffectual shove. "Like I said, scum. People like you always act like this. Such vile behaviour." He raised his drink, what appeared to be whiskey, and drank it in one go. "My mother is worth a million of you. Now, if you'll excuse me, I'd like to have a word with my sister. It's been a long time coming."

Chesney stalked away from her towards Nessa who picked up another sandwich and popped it in her mouth. Karen dragged a squealing Mum out of the pub, and everyone else swung their gazes round to see what would happen next.

Sod having an audience for this. Nessa jerked her head and led the way to her office. She wasn't about to air any dirty laundry in public, especially as she had to pretend to be on Chesney's side so she could save that woman tomorrow.

She sat behind her desk and gestured for him to sit opposite. Plate placed in front of her, she continued to eat to show him she wasn't about to be cowed or rushed. Marlborough had seemed to think Nessa was a female version of Dickie, and she wouldn't disabuse this lad of that. If they thought she'd go off on one at the flick of a switch like her father, that was to her advantage. Besides, she knew their secret, about selling drugs, so they'd do well to watch what they said around her. At least until the twins were brought in on it.

She drew one of the desk drawers open and produced a bottle of brandy and two glasses. She poured their measures and pushed one towards him.

"Welcome to our side of the family at last." Chesney gulped a few mouthfuls, not a flinch in sight. Was he fond of the booze? "Mum said you agreed to help us."

"I did, but only because we're related. You don't abandon family." *Liar.* "Well, unless it involves my mother. How are you holding up?"

"Gutted deep down, but what can you do? If you show emotion, people will home in on it, use it against you. We have to hide our feelings."

"Were you close to Dickie, then?"

Chesney's forehead ruffled. "Don't you call him Dad?"

"Not now I don't feel duty-bound, no. Our father never wanted me. I wasn't a boy, so…"

"I didn't realise that." He sounded genuinely concerned and a tad confused. "He was always telling us how loyal you are, how strong. Spoke highly of you, actually. I was under the impression you had a solid relationship."

"Shame he never said those things directly to me. All I got was verbal abuse and put down a lot. As for a solid relationship, err, no. We didn't get on. Still, that's all over now. So…why did you come? To put my mum in her place?"

"Hmm. She's badmouthed my mother over the years."

"Can you blame her?"

"No, but even if it's years later, if my mum's hurt, I fix it. I see you don't do the same for yours."

"We have very different upbringings and parents, me and you. The dad you knew wasn't the one I knew. My mother's a waste of space. Anyway, she's moving soon, up north, so that's something." She changed the subject. "How's your guest?"

He frowned, as if he didn't know what she referred to, then clicked his fingers. "I see what you did there. A very Dad move in disguising what you're really saying. She's okay. I've been injecting her with heroin to keep her quiet."

Nessa's stomach rolled over. So not only had he brought on the death of a baby and chained the woman up, he now plied her with drugs?

"Um, you need to be careful," she warned. "You don't want a fatal overdose on your hands. The baby being left in the church is bad enough, but if another body turns up? The police and pathologist might put two and two together if they twig and do a DNA test."

"Dad said you were smart."

"That's good of him."

Chesney didn't seem to pick up on her sarcasm. "Mum said you'll come to the office tomorrow and deal with the guest."

Nessa thought of the burner phone Marlborough had given her. In the notes app, she'd put the office address. "Yes. I'll get Susie to cover the pub for the day. Claim it's for bereavement reasons why I won't be around."

"Clever."

Hardly. "Is your mum having a few drinks of her own, a private wake?"

"Yeah, at the Crosshatch Arms."

"Right. Well…"

"I'd better get back." He gulped the rest of his drink, bashed the glass onto the desk, and stood. "See you in the morning, sis."

He walked out, and she stared at the door closing behind him.

Sis, my arse.

Chapter Two

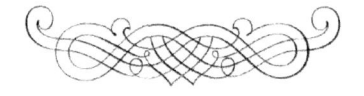

DI Janine Sheldon had tormented herself every day since the baby had been found — by coming here to view it. With no hits forthcoming on the DNA database, the body would be kept cold for a while longer in the hope that the mother came forward. It happened sometimes, guilt pushing them to confess they'd abandoned their child, or pressure from it being on the news. On the other hand, it could be detrimental, the mum feeling so bad about what she'd done that she couldn't take the pressure. Janine hoped the poor cow didn't do something stupid.

Jim, the pathologist, had named the child Luke on account of him being found in the church. This baby had affected the team so much more than other cases, children's deaths always hard to stomach.

Janine stared down at the scrappy mite. He was no more than nine inches from head to toe and weighed under a pound. *So* obviously premature. His mother must have cared for him, otherwise she wouldn't have wrapped him in a blanket, one Jim had noted came from Home Bargains, a black-and-white check type from the pet aisle—he had the same one for his cat. It was new, he thought, as it didn't have vast amounts evidence on it like it would had it been well-used. A couple of fibres had been picked up, though, perhaps from a carpet. Grey. Wiry. Janine still waited for the test results as to whether those fibres were from the boot of a car. If they got the make, they could hopefully find who was responsible.

Luke had still been bloody when discovered in front of the altar by the priest, the umbilical cord and placenta attached, a cowl on his head, the amniotic sac clinging on. Jim had cleaned him up after the post-mortem, of course he had, and dressed him in the tiniest blue sleepsuit and woolly hat he could find.

The lab results so far had been alarming. Luke would have been born addicted. Traces of cocaine had been detected in his system, as was alcohol. Jim estimated that despite Luke's size, the pregnancy had been at six months gestation. Had Luke gone to term, he may have only weighed four pounds, his growth so stunted it was criminal.

Janine had struggled with the mum taking the time to buy him a new blanket yet she'd endangered his life while he'd been inside her. It just showed how drugs had such a hold, where even though she'd been pregnant, she hadn't stopped. What kind of life did she lead if she took drugs and drank? She needed help, and Janine wanted to find her so she could get her looked after. Abandoning a baby under the age of two was a criminal offence in the UK, and Janine agreed with that, but she couldn't help but wonder about any extenuating circumstances.

The mother could be a minor, hooked on drugs and too afraid to tell anyone she'd been pregnant. Luke may have been born too early because of what she put into her body—and she may not have had any choice in what she snorted up her nose or sipped from a bottle. Too many horror stories sat in the files at the police station, and it wasn't a stretch to believe that the mother's life may be orchestrated by someone else. She could be in the sex trade and her captors set off the labour once they'd found out she'd been carrying a child. A pregnant woman was no good to them.

Yes, the abandonment was a criminal offence, but sometimes punishment for that wasn't warranted. On the other side of the coin, if she'd deliberately doped herself up and hadn't cared that Luke had come too early, that was a different matter.

Janine walked out, leaving the attendant to put the baby back into his cold bedroom, a drawer in a wall. Luke was perfect to look at, and it angered and saddened her that his life outside the womb hadn't had a chance to begin. Jim had said the lungs weren't formed enough for Luke to breathe, and even if he *had* breathed, going into an incubator would have been touch and go. He'd predicted Luke would have died anyway had he been alive when discovered.

In the car, she glanced across at Colin, her DS.

"Why do you keep doing this to yourself, going to visit him?" He slurped from his ever-present can of Pepsi Max.

"Because I do. We'll speak to the priest now he's got over the shock. He was a mess before."

"Weren't we all?"

"I'm annoyed we were told to leave him be for so long."

"Hmm, I did wonder why the boss said that. Maybe because it's a priest, he felt he had to cut him some slack."

"But he could have information we could have used way before now."

On the drive there, thoughts of the mother holding her baby while he died swirled around Janine's head. She hoped he'd had that comfort, at least, one small moment having his one and only cuddle, to have felt love before the angels took him. The grim alternative, him being born and left on the ground in an alley, didn't bear thinking about. Could that have been what happened, though? Had someone found him outside on their way home from the shops, taken the blanket they'd bought for their pet out of a bag, and carried him to the church?

With no CCTV around there, we'll never know.

The TV appeals hadn't worked. No one had come forward, so if a good Samaritan had done their bit, they'd either decided to remain anonymous or hadn't seen the news.

"We've got fuck all," she muttered.

"What was that?" Colin asked.

"Nothing, just moaning to myself."

"Want to share?"

"I wish we hadn't been put on the case. We usually deal with murder, and yes, Luke's death could well be that, but this isn't the kind of thing we do. It's affecting me so much that I'm going to ask the boss to put someone else in charge of it tomorrow. You also struggle, so I can't see you complaining if I do that."

"Nope. I've found this difficult."

Janine had nightmares about seeing the baby being pulled out of its mother, angry sex traffickers wanting to get rid of him, and she woke disorientated and crying. But she had Cameron now, the bodyguard the twins had assigned to her, a man she'd allowed into her heart. He held her in the night and calmed her. These new, horrific dreams had taken over the ones inspired by her past when she'd been known as Rusty, and she never thought she'd say she'd welcome *those* back instead. But they were better the devil she knew, familiar, and the ones with Luke were shocking and vivid, unpredictable.

She continued the journey, switching the radio on to take her mind away from that baby. His mother. And tried to kid herself that she'd walk away from the case tomorrow and leave it in someone else's hands.

Father Dublin, a young man annoyingly wafting around in white robes with a green stole, didn't appear to want to take them to his church office or sit on the pews to chat. Janine had requested that he lock the double front doors so they wouldn't be interrupted, and he busied himself flitting from a flower arrangement to a lectern to a stack of Bibles. He had the air of guilt hanging around him, and it smelled fouler than the mouldy, *old* scent in the air.

In the first pew, Janine glanced at Colin. Leaned close to whisper, "He knows something."

"Hmm. Stalling to get his story straight one last time?"

"I had a feeling that's why he didn't want to speak to us in depth when the baby was found."

Dublin had seemed too distraught to give much of a statement. He'd babbled about the baby being on the altar steps, and Janine had no reason not to believe him. He'd cried, crossed himself several times, and wailed that it had been God's will that the child had died, saying, "Too good for this world," and other things like that. The shock of seeing Luke in that blanket had skewed Janine's thought processes, and she'd backed off on her questioning. The DCI stepping in and telling them to leave the priest be had annoyed her, it wasn't right, but at last, here they were, days later, finally with the go-ahead to get some answers.

Having had enough of Dublin's behaviour, Janine called out, "Come and sit down. I'm sorry, but you're being rude, and the baby is the important thing here, not you tidying up. I understand how distressing this is, so I'll record the statement so you don't have to go through it all again, all right?"

Dublin seemed to glide over, his cheeks reddening. He linked his spindly, bulbous-knuckled fingers over his stomach, his short brown hair swept back. "I have a prayer meeting to get ready for at six. I won't let the parishioners down."

"But you're letting *Luke* down," Janine gritted out.

"Who?"

"The baby. He's been called Luke." Janine took a deep breath and set the recording device up. She said the usual verbiage then continued. "Father Dublin, while I realise it was a shock for you to find baby Luke, and I completely understand wanting to pretend it didn't happen, it did, and we *have* to find his mother. *She* also needs help. She could even be one of the people who worship here, which is why Luke was brought to your church."

He shook his head as if to refute that then stopped, realising he'd given himself away.

"What aren't you telling us?" she asked, eyes narrowed.

"Nothing." He made the sign of the cross. "I can't imagine anyone in my congregation would do such a thing."

"Are you saying Christians aren't capable of it?" Colin asked, uncharacteristically getting involved. He usually stood back and let Janine lead the way. It just proved how much Luke had affected him. "In my experience, some of the most hideous people have claimed to be Christian. Pardon me for saying so, but *anyone* is capable of *anything*, no matter which god they pray to, no matter how much they claim to be good."

"Yes, well, that's as may be," Dublin blustered, "but… I've prayed for Luke and his mother. This evening's prayer meeting is dedicated to his soul and entrance into Heaven, which is why it's so important I have everything ready in time. People want to mourn him, he's touched their hearts, and I want to be there for them, to help them through it."

"Luke's mother may not have been allowed to report her son's death to the proper authorities," Janine said. "She could be living a horrible life with horrible people, and while Luke being dead is an awful tragedy I will *never* forget, I have to concentrate on the living at the moment—his mum and/or anyone else involved. Talk me through it all, please. Your input could be invaluable. We've already let you give the brief facts last time we spoke, due to you being so 'upset', but now's the time to be more open about it. We can't wait any longer. It's been days."

Colin jumped in. "Do you know our boss?"

Dublin appeared startled. "Pardon?"

"Our boss." Colin gave the DCI's name. "Only, you've been given preferential treatment, allowed to have all this time without giving us a formal statement, which, to be frank, isn't the norm and isn't on."

"He comes here once a month on a Sunday, yes," Dublin said. "A good man."

"Why would he stall our investigation by preventing us from speaking to you?" Colin asked. "Did you ask him to tell us to back off?"

Janine nudged him. The DCI would hear all that on the recorded statement. Colin gave her a look that said he didn't give a shit. And maybe he didn't. He was seeing out the next wee while until his retirement, so what did *he* care about being reprimanded?

Dublin's cheeks turned even redder. "I asked for some space, yes. He believes this is the scenario of a teenager having a baby and panicking."

So why put us on the case? Why say it's murder?

Dublin glanced at the locked doors, as if he expected someone to bash them open and storm down the aisle. He kept his attention there for so long Janine turned to glance over her shoulder, then at him.

"Father Dublin?" she barked, her voice echoing, her annoyance showing. "What happened?"

"Right, right. I'd been in the vestry, changing out of my vestments, when I heard the church door open. It squeaks, as I'm sure you noticed when you came in. We haven't had that fixed as it serves as a signal that someone has arrived. We've had the odd homeless person coming in and trying to take the donation box, which we've now bolted down, and teenagers have caused problems."

Why is he stalling? "Could you keep on track, please?"

"Of course. I came out to see who it was, and a woman in one of those hoodies and blue jeans walked down the aisle carrying something in a checkered blanket. I couldn't see what it was at the time and—"

Janine almost exploded on him. "*Why* didn't you tell us this before?"

"I thought I did…"

"No, you said Luke was on the altar steps when you found him," Colin snapped. "That's what you told us *and* the PCs."

"But he was."

"*When*?" Janine clenched her fists.

"If you'd have let me finish…" Dublin's bottom lip wobbled. "This is all so distressing."

"I'm sure it is, but Luke's mother may be in even more distress, and you withholding that kind of information has put us on the back foot. Had we known a woman was involved, we might have found her by now."

"I'm terribly sorry…"

"Are you?" Janine hadn't meant to say that.

Had Dublin told the DCI about the woman? If so, why hadn't he passed that information on? None of this made sense.

"So what happened next?" she asked.

"I approached her and asked if I could help. She thrust the bundle at me and said I had to take care of it, the funeral. Sort it out. The woman handed me what I thought was folded paper, then rushed out. I put Luke on the altar steps—which is where he was when you arrived—and opened what turned out to be an envelope. It contained money, which I guessed was to pay for the funeral. I went back to him and had a proper look and…" Dublin gasped as though distraught. "He was…he was purple, and he had blood on him."

I know. "What then?"

"I rang the police. Said a baby had been murdered. Two men in uniform came, then you two."

"Why did you think he'd been murdered?"

"Abortion is murder."

Why would he think Luke had been aborted?

Janine stiffened. She wouldn't allow herself to be drawn into the pro-life debate. "That is a matter of opinion, and he may not have been aborted. Did she tell you he was?"

He muttered something, clearly agitated. Janine had the awful feeling that for whatever reason, Dublin and the DCI had cooked up a story between them. Or was the priest lying, keeping a secret all to himself?

Finally, he said, "Um, no?"

Why phrase that as a question? "So you assumed she had. Why did you do that?"

"Your boss suggested that must have been what happened. He said people do that often."

What the hell? "What did the woman look like?"

"Blonde, long hair. Young, about fifteen?"

Janine closed her eyes for a moment then opened them to find Dublin had shifted his gaze from the door to her. "How did she seem?"

He frowned. "What do you mean?"

"Was she in good health? On drugs?"

Dublin thought for a few seconds. "Yes, I suppose she was."

"Which are you referring to?"

"Drugs."

"In what way did she make you think she was on them?"

Nervous, he fiddled with his fingers. "Ah…um…she had spots around her mouth, and her eyes were red."

"Maybe she had acne and had been crying because, you know, her baby had died and she'd had to leave him here. Her parents may not have known about the pregnancy, which could have been a terrible secret she had to carry around with her. How else did she look?"

"Spaced out."

"That could be because she'd just given birth without any pain relief. I hear it's incredibly agonising." Her sarcasm floated between them. "Are you *sure* she was a drug user? It's important that you're honest and not just telling us something we want to hear." *Or what you've been told to say.*

"She wasn't right, put it that way."

Colin cleared his throat. "Did you not wonder how someone so young had money to give to you?"

Dublin shrugged. "I thought the father had given it to her. Perhaps he was an older man…"

"How much was there?" Janine asked.

"Five hundred."

She raised her eyebrows. "And where is it?"

Dublin blushed harder. "I don't know."

"What?"

"I *don't know*. I put it on the altar steps with the baby, and then it was gone after the police came."

"So you're saying one of the officers *stole* it?"

"No! Maybe they took it as evidence."

"Did you tell them, before we arrived, that you'd been given the cash?"

"I don't remember."

Colin snorted. "No money has been logged at the station."

"But that's not my fault!" Dublin once again wafted away. He knelt in front of the altar, mumbling prayers.

Janine looked at Colin and whispered, "Fucking prick."

Colin nodded. "He's lying."

Janine stared at Dublin's back. "What does God think about perjury, Father?"

He paused. "It's a sin."

"So why have you committed it?"

"I…I haven't."

"So do you swear your statement is true and correct?"

"Yes."

"Then I'll remember that for later. It will be typed up, and an officer will come by for you to read and sign it. I hope for your sake you're not lying to us. Interview ended at four-fifteen p.m." She finished signing it off and stalked up the aisle.

Dublin scuttled after her and opened the doors.

Colin joined her outside. "I don't even feel bad saying this about a member of the clergy, but what a fucking dickhead. He's bullshitting about that money."

"Yep, and who knows what else?" Janine inhaled through her nose to calm her temper. "Let's hope he isn't bullshitting about the woman as well."

Janine couldn't let this slide. She stood in the DCI's office and stared him down after telling him what they'd learned.

"Ah." He leaned back in his chair. "I wasn't aware of any woman handing the baby over. The only reason I gave him a few days to get his head together is because I honestly believe this is an open-and-shut case. Young girl has baby, panics, and dumps it."

"It doesn't make sense why me and Colin are on the case then, as if it's murder."

"I had orders for us to investigate it as such."

"So your boss doesn't agree with your suspicions?"

"No."

"Rightly so. This could be any number of scenarios. That baby could have been forced out of her by some gang. Are you guilty of wanting to brush all this aside because you go to that church?"

He glared at her. "Watch your tone."

"Do you see why I'm upset, though, sir?"

"Yes." He sighed. "I agree, it *does* seem odd that Dublin didn't say about the woman at the time of discovery. Maybe he's hiding something, much as I wish he wasn't. All I'm *guilty* of, as you put it, is letting him have some space and believing a girl panicked and had to get rid of the child—granted, I shouldn't have treated him any differently to anyone else had they found the body. We've seen it so many times before. Now you've come to me with all this, I'm inclined to lean towards your way of thinking."

"For a moment there, I thought you were a bent copper," she said. A hypocrite, because *she* was one. "I'm going to proceed as if Dublin isn't a priest. If he's shielding someone and we find out, I *will* bring him in no matter what it looks like."

He sighed. "I apologise. I'm snowed under and wanted this wrapped up quickly. Off our hands."

She saw him in a different light, and it saddened her. "This is a *baby*, sir. A tiny little boy who needs justice. We can't just sweep this under the rug. I want to know who that woman is and why she did this. It could be so much more than an abandonment."

"Go ahead. I'll beat myself up in private, once you've gone."

"Good."

She walked out, pleased with herself, although that soon dissipated into anger.

Dublin had lied.

Why?

Chapter Three

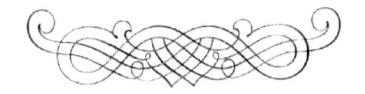

Father Dublin took his vestments off and hung them on a hook on the back of the door. The vestry, chilly no matter the season, seemed to close in on him, the walls shrinking. A sense of foreboding stole over him, but he brushed it away. The church always felt ominous when he was the only one here, and his feelings were nothing more than a silly, fanciful thought that he wasn't alone. He'd like to think it was

God, showering him with His presence, but more often than not he believed it to be the Devil, trying to infiltrate this sanctuary and pull him over to the dark side.

He shivered and swiped the sweat from his forehead, glad today was all but over. He loved his job, his calling, but some days he found dealing with people a little too much. He'd discovered he only had a limited amount of time and energy where he could cope with everyone's problems, and more and more lately, the troubles in his corner of the East End had seemed to quadruple. All those coming to the church foodbank, their bills sky-high, their bellies empty, growling. Too many came here in unkempt clothing, their hair greasy, their skin with an unwashed sheen. He wished he could help them all, but sadly, he couldn't.

He ran a soup kitchen every Wednesday. Once upon a time it had only been the homeless who'd taken advantage of the hot food and a bread roll, but more and more he'd seen others here, people who lived in houses they couldn't afford to heat. He donated a lot of his wages, living frugally so he could buy more vegetables for the soup, which Hazel, one of his aides, cooked on Tuesday nights in her big urn. She was a chef in the Crosshatch Arms on the other side of this housing estate, where more well-to-do people lived, and the landlord allowed her to use the facilities to help those in need.

Then there were the rich, who swanned in here and donated cash openly, perhaps hoping that their benevolence would be witnessed, therefore, it proved they were 'good' people. The same as those who filmed themselves giving money to the homeless and putting it on social media. Show-offs he couldn't abide, especially when those down on their luck saw the banknotes being put into the slot of the donation box one by one. Yes, the money was needed to maintain the church, but he often wished he had the bottle to put some of that cash aside and hand it out to those who were desperate.

That would be a sin, though. Thou shalt not steal.

One of the front doors squeaked, the sound echoing, and in his suit, he rushed out of the vestry to see who had come. He selfishly hoped it was someone who wanted to pray quietly, that they didn't want his advice. It had been a long day, evening drawing in, and with no services tonight, he'd been looking forward to going home and curling up with a book.

A man in a hooded, dark-navy sweatshirt, his head dipped, came down the aisle carrying something in a black-and-white-checked blanket. Dublin couldn't see what it was and thought perhaps it was a cat struck down on the road in front of St Matthew's. While he felt for the poor creature, it wasn't his job to contact a vet.

He told himself off for his uncharitable thought.

"Can I help you?" he asked.

The man came closer. "You've got to sort this child's funeral."

Child?

Dublin, startled by those words, blinked, trying to see the man's face. The hood obscured the top half—was that sunglasses he had on?—but the bottom showed a thin, mean mouth and what he'd heard called a glass jaw, which would have the limited ability to absorb a punch should someone strike it. He judged him to be young, a teenager maybe, going by the slender build and the smooth, unwrinkled skin.

The unwanted guest shoved the bundle at Dublin who clutched it to his chest. Staring down at it didn't reveal a child's face, the folds of the blanket covering it. And how could this be *a child? It weighed next to nothing.*

The man tucked paper or something between the blanket and Dublin's chest. "There's enough cash for a cheap one."

Dublin momentarily forgot what a 'cheap one' would refer to, then the word FUNERAL *barged into his mind. He swallowed. The lad's rough East End accent seemed fake, as though this person disguised their own. Was he someone Dublin knew?*

"What...how did this child come to die?"

"Abortion gone wrong. My girlfriend asked me to do it. I can't go in the nick. Been there before. She's only fourteen, see. I'm twenty. I'd get done for her being underage as well as trying to get rid of the baby. We panicked when we found out she was preggers. Her dad would go mental if he found out."

Dublin pondered that. Many a time young girls had come in to ask his advice on this very subject. He'd told them to go home and tell their parents, as abortion was a sin and they must atone for it. God wanted these babies on earth, otherwise the eggs and sperm wouldn't have connected.

He considered whether he was dealing with someone who had mental health issues. Honestly, this bundle, there was nothing to it, so it might not be a baby at all.

But he mentioned an abortion, so... Oh, dear God in Heaven, give me the strength to get through this.

"How old is the child?" Dublin asked.

"Think my bird was about four months pregnant. That's what she looked like anyway. She's skinny, so I couldn't tell."

"But if she's your girlfriend, surely you'd know."

The lad's hand shot out and gripped Dublin's neck. Squeezed. That thin mouth grew even thinner with the effort he put into the grip. The move was so violent Dublin almost dropped the bundle, so he held it tighter, mindful he might squash it.

"Listen to me, you fucking do-gooder prick. Stop asking questions and just get that kid a proper burial, all right? It wasn't his fault he died. I feel bad, just so you know, and he has to be buried so he gets into Heaven."

So he has a conscience? He believes in God?

Dublin's heartrate increased, his chest taut where he couldn't draw in sufficient air. "Please, could you let go? You're hurting me." His words came out as strangled as his neck.

The hand released. "Not one word about me being here, got it? Say the kid was left on the altar or something. If people know this was me, they'll be after me. I'll end up dead."

What a quandary. And could Dublin believe him? Really? "I have to inform the police about the baby. I can't just organise a funeral. There are protocols to follow. I'd be breaking the law if I didn't tell anyone, and breaking my vows to God."

Thin Mouth sighed. Paced. Slapped at his head.

"I can see you're troubled," Dublin said.

"Of course I fucking am. Jesus, this wasn't supposed to happen." He kicked the side of a pew. "Fine, call the police, but you tell them I came here, and I'll come back for you, understand? Slit your holy throat."

Dublin nodded, frightened out of his mind when a flick-knife appeared out of Thin Mouth's pocket. "Okay. Just go. I'll fix everything."

"I mean it. He needs *a funeral. And one word…"*

"I…I understand. Please, just leave."

*"*Don't *ring the cops until I've been gone five minutes."*

"All right, all right."

The lad fled, one of the doors banging shut behind him. The sound reverberated, a bind on Dublin's nerves, coiling them and bringing tears to his eyes. On shaky legs, he took the bundle to the altar steps and laid it down. The paper, an envelope he realised now, fell on top of the blanket. Dublin pushed it aside and peeled back a fold of fleece material. A tiny, tiny face appeared, and he recoiled in shock. So purple, so bloody, the features so small. Eyes closed. Mouth a miniature rosebud. He swallowed, crying, his tears hot, angry that he'd been put in this position. He covered the face up and lifted the envelope.

He ignored the voice of God in his mind and ripped open the seal. Twenty-pound notes, which he counted. Two thousand pounds. This baby was gone, there was no helping it now, and a funeral would be provided by the state. The poor parishioners, though, they could do with that money.

Maybe that was why the man had come here. Sad as this baby's death was, the tot may have just been a vessel in which to bring the money to Dublin. That would feed a lot of families. He could stock up the church's foodbank over the course of next week, claim that more bags had been donated than usual, when in fact, he'd bought them himself. Better that the cash went to those in need than an aborted baby.

That was right, wasn't it?

"Thou shalt not steal," God whispered.

Again Dublin ignored Him. He rushed into the vestry and hid the envelope in an urn. Said a quick prayer for forgiveness. Picked up the phone and dialled nine-nine-nine.

"Which emergency do you require?"

Dublin sighed. "I'd like to report a murder."

Dublin had felt pushed into giving the detectives more of a story. He'd panicked at DI Sheldon's tone, her staring at him as if she knew he'd lied. He'd switched it from a man to a woman, which would be more plausible anyway, and hadn't meant to blurt about the money.

He'd opened a can of worms that should have been left shut. Sheldon would dig and dig until she uncovered the truth, and as for her DS…that man was unsettling.

Should I contact their boss? Explain? Say I was do upset at the time we spoke that I hadn't mentioned the 'woman'?

And the money. He'd already spent the majority of it. Now Sheldon knew it had existed, would she poke into it, think he'd stolen it, and send officers to the shops he'd been in? No, that was silly. He was being paranoid.

But what if he wasn't?

Dublin sank to his knees in front of the altar and prayed.

Chapter Four

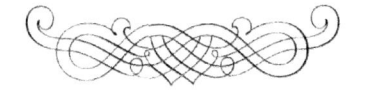

All of her life, Pippa hadn't belonged. It was hard to describe, she couldn't put her finger on why, but a square peg in a round hole wasn't something she enjoyed being. Her parents found her excess to requirements, or maybe that was just her perception. They didn't seem to know whether she was in the room or not, and she'd often thought they shouldn't have had her. They liked to party and had left her with a

babysitter a lot, rolling in at three a.m., laughing about their evening, then the bed squeaked for ages.

She'd had an imaginary friend — well, a teddy, and she'd made up a voice for it to talk back to her. Bear had been her constant companion for as long as she could remember, and he still sat on her bed to this day, his fur a little matted, his clothes raggedy. A lonely childhood, if not for Bear. How could her parents not have noticed she'd relied on him to get her through the years? Hadn't they cared?

She didn't want kids herself. Couldn't risk realising she'd made a mistake in having one. Couldn't put a child through how she'd felt.

The same feeling could be said for her job. She was there but not, working but unnoticed, a busy bee who droned in the background while three of the other employees had made friends and gossiped, laughing about the nights out they'd shared. She'd never been invited, perhaps because she didn't push herself forward and hint that she'd like to join them. Or maybe, like with her parents, she wasn't seen.

Maybe it was time she put herself out there, but the problem was, could she stomach more rejection? She didn't earn much, and they did — and they had parents who supplemented their income. Flash clothes, shoes, handbags, posh makeup, and plenty of cash to spend getting pissed up or eating out. Her circumstances marked her out as different, so they likely didn't want someone in their circle who shopped off the rack, skint more often than not. If she hung around with them, she'd never keep up.

Unless she could get a credit card.

Fiona, a blonde, cackled at something Lillibet said, the conspiratorial looks they gave each other speaking of shared secrets and in-jokes. Pippa stared, envious, and jealous, the green-eyed monster rearing its heavy head. Theresa shot over to their desks and got in on the conversation.

Pippa glanced at Stephanie, the other pariah in the office, whose desk was next to hers.

"We should go out on our own," Stephanie said.

Pippa gawped at her. Was she for real? Like Pippa would want to spend time with that frumpy cow. She should have felt bad for thinking that, but she didn't. Sick of always being the one rejected, to have been asked out by a nerd, of all people, was offensive.

"Err, no," Pippa said.

Stephanie eyed her, as if she were shit on her shoe, and it was an unsettling moment. Pippa eyed her back, pissed off with being put in this position. Why was it always those she didn't want to be seen dead with who approached her? Why wasn't she popular?

Stephanie's whole demeanour changed. She brought her top half up straight, and her eyes held a hard glint. "For someone who hasn't exactly got a line of people asking her to go out for drinks, you really are a trumped-up bitch."

Pippa stared. Put like that, Stephanie had a point, but who the fuck did she think she was? And did she hide her true self under that simpering veneer she used when dealing with Mr Ford, their boss? It bloody well looked like it. Pippa couldn't get over the words that had come out of Stephanie's mouth. How she'd gone from the office wallflower to a raging dragon.

"Excuse me?" Pippa's face grew red, the skin prickling from the heat of mortification. "Speak for yourself. You only asked me because they don't want to know you either. I'm a last resort for you."

"I asked you because I felt sorry for you, but whatever. You think what you like."

"Sorry for me?"

"Hmm. I've got friends, they're just not in this office, and they'd have been fine with you tagging along with me, but as you clearly don't want to take the hand of friendship, maybe you should just go and fuck yourself. Go back to your lonely little life."

Pippa got up, unable to stand being subjected to a boatload of truth. How had Stephanie perceived her so clearly? And who knew she had a set of balls on her like that? Pippa would have sworn the woman was scared of her own shadow. It just went to show you couldn't judge a book an' all that. The spite had been a bit of a shock to be honest. Was this how people felt when Pippa gave them the sharp edge of her tongue?

She stormed to the toilets, locking herself in a cubicle. If she was even being treated this way by the office dweeb, something was seriously wrong.

Pippa took her phone out and Googled a credit card, the one where people with a crap rating always got accepted. The interest rates were high, but she'd have to cope with that. If she could just get a couple of grand to kit herself out with nice clothes and pay for a few nights out, Fiona, Lillibet, and Theresa might view her differently. They might let her into their clique. She might belong.

She waited for the acceptance notice, shaking when it informed her she'd been successful. The card would arrive within five working days, so she sat for a moment to imagine going to the high-end charity shop where rich people donated clothing and shoes. She'd get a lot for her money there, and no one would know they'd been purchased secondhand.

She left the toilet and returned to her desk, making eye contact with Stephanie, although she wished she hadn't. The woman smirked and turned her nose up in the air, then smiled to herself, maybe thinking mean things. Pippa sat, humiliation and anger rushing through her, and she wanted to run, to not be there anymore, to hide away from what she imagined was her shame plastered all over her hot face.

It took an immense amount of effort to concentrate on work. She sensed Stephanie glancing at her every so often, and the other three opposite seemed to have picked up on the tension. They'd been busy talking earlier when Stephanie had delivered her spiteful barbs, so that was something. If they'd overheard, surely they'd have stepped in and said something to defend Pippa.

Lunchtime rolled around, and she couldn't get out of there fast enough. The trio would be going to the Old Woodshed over the road for bar food, and Stephanie usually ate at her desk, a takeaway delivered. Pippa always left the building to walk down an alleyway then sit on one of the numerous benches positioned around a mouldy, moss-covered stone fountain. She brought a packed lunch, always embarrassed she had to do that. Sandwiches, an apple, and tea in a small flask, the meal so obviously hinting that she couldn't afford to eat out. Mum said it was sensible, that saving money meant she could spend it on other things, but didn't her parents get the fact that because three quarters of her wages went on rent and utilities, she couldn't afford sod all? It wasn't like they were offering for her to move back in. They'd given her notice to leave as soon as she'd left college, like she was a tenant, not their daughter.

Tears stung. Maybe she should find another job that paid better. Or get a second one in the evenings. But she'd barely have any free time then, and what sort of life was that? Tired of scraping by to make ends meet, of her dreams being shattered—the ones where she'd stupidly thought that being an adult would be easier than being a child—she let the tears fall down her cheeks.

An old man ambled along, a cheeky pigeon landing on his shoulder. He reminded her of the bird lady in that Home Alone *film, clearly a tramp or at least down on his luck. Again, she should have felt something, empathy or whatever, but all that went through her was a streak of unfairness that she hadn't got the things in life she wanted. Dad would say she was an ungrateful cow, that there were so many people out there who'd be chuffed with what she had: a rented flat that was warm and dry; a secure job; clothes on her back, shoes on her feet. But she didn't have anyone to laugh with. No one to share her worries with. Dad had Mum, but who did* she *have?*

The old man sat beside her, and she shifted along a bit. He didn't smell too great.

"Got a chip on your shoulder, have you?" he asked.

Did she? Was that how she came across?

She ignored him.

"Thought so," he went on. "You can tell a mile off. People like you don't associate with the likes of me. And that's okay, because people like me are tired of people like you. There are some who are nice, I'll give them that. Buying us sandwiches, giving us a few quid for a hot coffee. But others, not so much. Remember, we're all one pay cheque away from it all going wrong."

She took her lunch out of her bag and passed it to him. That was all he wanted anyway, wasn't it? He wasn't speaking to her to be kind. She even put the flask on the bench between them. He could keep it, she didn't want it back if his manky mouth had been on it.

God, she sounded so cruel but couldn't seem to help herself. Every thought went negative and selfish lately. Google said she might have depression.

"Are you sure you want to part with your food?" he asked. "I mean, it's not going to make me get up and

walk away, you giving me this. And doing this one good thing won't erase all the bad."

He was giving her the creeps, knowing how she felt inside.

"So why are *you sitting here, then?" She stared ahead at a flock of pigeons accosting some bloke in a suit eating his McDonald's.*

"I get a sense about people, and you're unhappy." He bit into her cheese and onion sandwich. "It's coming off you in waves. Want to talk about it?"

She did, actually, and an old man was better than no one at all. So what if she was using him as a sounding board. She'd bet hardly anyone spoke to him anyway, the scruffy bastard, so he ought to be grateful she was.

"I've got no one who gives a shit about me," she said.

"Do you know why?"

She shrugged. "No."

"Maybe it's the vibes you're letting off."

She stiffened. Dad had said similar once. That she was unapproachable and held herself in check all the time. Was it any wonder when she'd drifted through life unseen? Yet this old boy had seen her. Had apparently seen right through her, for fuck's sake.

She took a deep breath. "What vibes?"

"Like you're better than everyone else. But no one's better than anyone. We all bleed red, we all cry, we all have worries. No one's superior just because they have money or a roof over their heads. What you put out is what you get back."

"So you're saying I'm treated like shit because I do the same to other people?"

"You said it, not me…" He munched on the rest of the sandwich.

"I don't know how to be any different."

"Then learn. If you've got a bit of compassion to give, it goes a long way. Makes you and the person you're with feel better. Smile more, and people will smile back. You'll seem more approachable. At the moment, it's like you've got a wall around you."

"Yet here you are…"

He chuckled and tossed her apple from hand to hand. *"What have I got to lose by speaking to you? Most folks ignore me, they think I'm scum, so when someone actually answers me, I call that my win for the day. I feel seen. That I matter. Maybe you should do the same. You're not doing too badly at the minute, you're being polite enough to me, even though you're only tolerating me, wishing I'd go away, but it's a start. You sit here every workday, on your own, I've noticed that. And even if people sit beside you, there's no chatting. Maybe try striking up a conversation with someone tomorrow. You might be surprised by what happens. Friends aren't made by being silent with a face like a slapped arse."*

"So I need to reevaluate how I act, is that it? Why does it have to be me? Why can't people be nicer to me instead?"

"I just was. You've responded, which is more than your usual. You haven't been struck down for doing so either. The world didn't end. Lighten up. Things could be so much worse. You could be homeless, a cardboard box as your blanket." He chuckled at the irony, popped the apple in his pocket, and rose. "Sip your tea and have a think."

He rustled off, taking his stench with him. He hadn't touched the flask, so she poured herself a drink and pondered what he'd said. Maybe he was right, it was *her who needed to change, but she was so miserable half the time that she couldn't see past the black cloud that always dogged her.*

She got angry on the walk back to the office. He'd hit the nail on the head, and she didn't like it. She'd closed herself off to avoid being hurt, and in return, she'd hurt other people.

The afternoon dragged on. Stephanie got up and went over to Fiona's desk, bending low to speak to her.

Although she held a file, she didn't open it, and Pippa was convinced they spoke about something else, about her, especially when Stephanie glanced over and smirked again.

That's it, I've had enough of this shit. Sod what that old man said.

"If you've got something to say about me," Pippa snapped loudly, "say it to my face."

Stephanie rose to her full height. "Why do you think it's about you?"

"You just smirked at me."

"Did I?" Stephanie shrugged. "If I did, it's because you fucked up on this job and I wanted to ask Fiona how to approach you, seeing as you're so prickly. I could have gone to Mr Ford and told him, but I was doing you a courtesy by trying to get it fixed so our boss doesn't have to see it."

Fiona shook her head, as though that wasn't the reason Stephanie had gone over there at all. What was going on?

Embarrassment smeared itself all over Pippa's cheeks. "You should have come to me, not Fiona."

"What, and get short shrift? I mean, you're being snappy now, so…"

Pippa got up and went over there. "Show me the file and where I went wrong."

Stephanie smiled. "Please…"

"Please." Pippa ground her teeth. She wanted to punch this woman's lights out but couldn't afford to lose her job. Why was her life so hard? Why couldn't she have an easy ride for a change?

Stephanie placed the file on the desk and opened it, pointing to a paragraph. "There."

Pippa read it. Christ, she had *fucked up. She'd have to swallow her pride, much as she hated to. "Thank you for finding that."*

Stephanie sniffed and returned to her desk.

Fiona whispered, "She's only being catty because you knocked her back earlier—yes, we heard it all. A while back she asked if she could hang around with us, but we declined. She's taking it out on you. She was making a point to me, not asking how to approach you. Watch her, she's a crafty bitch. We don't want anything to do with her unless it's for work."

"And you feel the same about me?"

Fiona's eyebrows lifted. "I didn't realise you wanted to be friends with us. You've always seemed so quiet and closed off. If you do, then meet us at The Bar on Saturday about eight. We're getting drunk in a pub crawl then going clubbing."

Pippa almost gave the excuse that she couldn't go, she didn't have the money, but she could use some of the rent and put it back from the credit card when it arrived. She had a nice enough outfit, one she kept for best, so that would do.

"Okay, that'd be great."

She went to her desk and read the paragraph, double-checking for more errors. Then a thought struck her. On the computer, she scanned her original work, just to be sure.

The mistake wasn't there.

So angry she couldn't see straight, she swung her chair to face Stephanie. "You doctored my report." She jabbed a thumb at her monitor. "There's my original work, look. It's correct."

That infernal smirk lifted Stephanie's rosy-apple cheeks. "That's what happens when you cross me. You'd do well to remember that."

To stop herself from launching off her chair and beating the shit out of her, Pippa printed out the original page and took the file to the boss. What should she do in future, though? Pippa always had to send her work to Stephanie who then read through it and handed it to Mr Ford. What if she wasn't as lucky next time and a deliberate error made it through?

If she said sorry and acted like she meant it, would Stephanie be nicer in the future?

"Just be polite to me," Stephanie said, as if reading her mind. "I don't put up with people being rude, I tend to want to get my own back, and that's never good for the other person concerned."

Now, more than ever, Pippa felt like she didn't fit in. She glanced over at Fiona who had listened to the whole exchange. As had Theresa and Lillibet. Fiona switched her attention to her monitor, and within seconds, an email alert pinged.

Pippa opened the new message.

From: Fiona Bainbridge
To: Pippa King

Meet us after work at the Old Woodshed. We need to talk.

Chapter Five

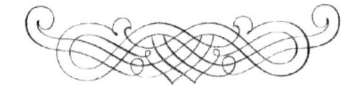

Pippa sweated beside the office radiator she'd been chained to, but it wasn't from the heat as it hadn't been switched on. She'd come down from the high Chesney had given her hours before and wished she was dead. It had been a long night, and now the sun nipped in around the edges of the blind, she wondered if today would be her last. The same thought she'd had every morning she'd woken up here, alone. But *they* would be here soon, ready to conduct business. Or maybe they wouldn't, seeing as another family member would be coming.

She'd learned a lot by listening. Some would say she'd learned too late, seeing as she'd cast aside that old man's advice and gone her own way.

Pippa had been fed and given water, chaperoned to the toilet when Miss Marlborough was here. Mother and son went outside to hand drugs over to whoever had come to buy them instead of letting them in, Pippa left indoors by herself. She had been one of those people so recently, able to walk away with her fix, but that last time…

It had all gone so wrong, and here she was, trapped, with no way to let anyone know where she was. Marlborough always stuffed a cloth in her mouth so she couldn't shout for help and only took it out when she gave her water from a bottle, food, or wanted Pippa to verbally respond. Chesney kept her topped up with H, enough to keep her silent, her mind sluggish, so it wasn't as if they had to worry.

This morning, though, she was alert.

The threat of being killed would do that to you.

She still bled from having the baby. Chesney said he'd been called Luke by the police and that they were searching for her. They wanted to do her for child abandonment, and he reckoned she'd be looking at a long stretch for that. Except *she* hadn't abandoned him, *he* had.

When he'd shoved her and she'd landed on her stomach, a massive wave of pain sweeping through her, she'd shouted that she'd phone the coppers on them, get them in the shit for being dealers. She wished she hadn't. Her baby would still be inside her if she'd kept her thoughts to herself. But her stupid big mouth had let her down, and now there would be no freedom.

Someone was coming today to murder her. Chesney's sister. Marlborough had seemed to take great pleasure in telling Pippa that. If this Nessa was anything like the other two, Pippa had no hope. Mother and son, a spiteful pair if ever she'd seen one, so God knew what the third family member was like.

Once again, she was the outcast. Alone. Her pimp, Crook, had been the only one to make her feel special. At first. He'd be wondering where she was, likely spouting off to all and sundry that she'd done a runner, shirked her duties, losing him money. He'd set up something similar to Debbie's Corner, although it wasn't in full view like hers but tucked down a narrow street. Pippa had stood there many a night, shitting herself in case a nasty punter came along, of which she'd serviced many. Some blokes took out their shame on her, as if it was *her* fault they'd chosen to sleep with a sex worker. Others just liked it rough.

She sighed, pushing away the memories.

Not only were the police searching for her, but Crook would have sent his men out, too. This was one time Pippa wished they'd find her so the Marlboroughs got a kicking. She wished she'd never needed money before she'd walked this path, wished she'd never met Crook, but at the time he'd been the answer to all of her worries.

Until he'd revealed who he really was.

The key going in the office door had her sitting upright, her heart fluttering, her bladder protesting. Marlborough, all in black, came in holding a bulging Tesco carrier bag which she dumped on the desk with the single key on a teddy ring. Pippa thought of Bear, sitting on her bed, and she had the mad urge to cuddle him for comfort.

Marlborough locked the door, totally ignoring Pippa, and got on with sticking the kettle on. She took her jacket off and hung it on the coatstand beside the door. Fiddled behind the blind to open the window.

Pippa welcomed that. She was too hot, and the stuffy air smelled of staleness. Like the old man at the fountain. She cleared her parched throat to get a response, but Marlborough swanned over to the kitchen station and took three cups out of a cupboard. Hers, Chesney's, and Nessa's, most likely.

Eventually, she spun and faced Pippa, all smiles. "Morning! Today is the day you get out of this mess and we can go back to normal."

Pippa's stomach rolled in surprise excitement. They'd changed their minds and were letting her go? Or had Crook found out where she was and made a deal with them?

Marlborough smiled wider. "Death is a way out, isn't it?"

Death's what I came here to achieve in the first place, but you refused to help me. You fucked it all up.

Marlborough came over, crouched, and took the cloth from Pippa's mouth. "I'd like to assure you it'll be quick, but I'm not sure on that. I don't know what Nessa's capable of. If she's like her father, she might draw it out. Get her pound of flesh for kicks. We'll soon see. She'll be here in a bit." She undid the chains from the radiator and helped Pippa to stand. "Oh, hang on."

Marlborough turned and, leaving Pippa standing there with the long, heavy chains dangling from the manacles on her wrists, walked to the desk and ferreted in the Tesco bag. "I bought you breakfast. Your last meal. I'd have asked you what you preferred, like they do on death row, but decided you didn't deserve that privilege." She tittered.

Pippa stared. Clenched her hands together. Anger belted through her at how this woman, this evil, *evil* cow could find this funny. None of this was. Pippa had been kept here for days on end, mourning her son—which had come as a total surprise—listening to their prattle, looking for a way out, desperate in her lucid moments, fucked up in the drugged ones. Her dreams had tormented her with the baby as the star, Pippa running, running, running, trying to find him, sensing him near but never locating him.

And this woman was *amused*?

Maybe this is what I deserve. I'm a horrible person.

Pippa tiptoed over to her captor slowly so the chains didn't clink together and rattle. She swung her arms, the thick-linked chains slapping onto the side of Marlborough's head. The woman staggered to the left, screaming in shock, and Pippa followed, swinging wildly, the chains making brutal contact again. Marlborough went down on her knees, clutching her head, her back to Pippa.

An angry snarl roaring out of her, Pippa rushed forward and kicked the bitch in the temple, hopefully doing a bit of damage. The move reminded her of the past, when she hadn't wanted to kick someone, but today, yes, she fucking well did. She kicked again, Marlborough groaning, disorientated. At the sound of the kettle clicking off, Pippa took her chance and grabbed it. She hesitated for a few seconds, unsure if she could burn someone, then, when Marlborough planted her hands on the floor and pushed her torso up, Pippa poured.

Steaming water splashed onto the cow's head and cascaded down one side of her face. Marlborough's screams seemed to fill the office, and she tried to stand, but the need to cover her cheek took over. Pippa moved the kettle to the other side and let the water do its work there, conscious she didn't have much time. Chesney usually arrived half an hour after his mother.

She dropped the empty kettle on the floor and snatched up the key Marlborough had casually dropped on the desk. Shaking, she shoved it in the lock and twisted. Yanked the door open. Fresh air had never tasted or felt so good. She ran, the chains slapping and curling around her legs at first, so she held them halfway down to make them shorter. She got to the main road a street away, worried Chesney would drive by and see her. Capture her and take her back. Small businesses lined the road, warehouses, a petrol station, and she headed there, attention darting all over the place in search of someone to help her.

A car came towards her, and she stiffened, her heart rate scattering. But she soon relaxed. It wasn't Chesney's familiar black SUV but a white car. It slowed. So did Pippa because a woman drove it.

The car stopped. The window wound down.

"Are you all right, love?" Kind eyes, a forty-something lady old enough to be Chesney's mother let alone his sister. This wasn't Nessa.

Pippa shook her head. Did she *look* all right, for fuck's sake? "I need the hospital."

"Get in. I'll take you."

She's a safe bet, isn't she?

Pippa ran round to the passenger side, conscious the sanitary pad between her legs hadn't been changed for hours. She opened the door and dipped her head to say, "I'm bleeding." She gestured to her groin.

The woman frowned, then her face changed into an expression of understanding. "Oh. Shit. It's okay. Everything will be all right, I promise."

Pippa got in and put her seat belt on, fighting the chains all the way. The woman drove off, round the corner, then parked outside a row of houses.

"What…what are you doing?" Pippa asked, unclipping the belt, ready to bolt.

"I need to tell the twins about this. They've got this clinic. You're better off going there if you're who I think you are. A hospital means too many questions. The Marlboroughs kept you, didn't they?"

"Who *are* you?"

"I'm Nessa, and I was just on my way to—"

Pippa grabbed the door handle.

Nessa gripped her wrist. "Listen to me. I might be Chesney's sister, but whatever they've told you, I'm not going to hurt you, all right? I swear, I was coming to get you, then telling The Brothers what's been going on. The police have been looking for you for *days*, love. It's been on the news and everything."

She sounded so sincere.

Can I trust her?

Pippa swallowed. "I can't take much more. If you're lying…"

"I'm not. You can get out of the car if you like, while I phone them. I'll put it on speaker so you can hear what's going on. I'm not the enemy here. If you want those two dealt with, this is the best way to go. *I* want them dealt with for reasons of my own. We've *both* got a beef."

Pippa got out. The swift bombardment of information had her confused, not knowing which way to turn. Run or stay? But the worry that Chesney would drive along sent her back into the car. She slunk down in the seat and closed her eyes as Nessa jabbed at her phone screen. Prayed this woman was on the level. Hoped luck had finally shone down on her.

"All right, Nessa," one of the twins said, gruff and annoyed. "What the fuck's going on that you're ringing us at this time of the morning?"

"I've found the woman, the mother of the abandoned baby."

"*What?*"

"I'll explain later, but people will be looking for her, not the good kind. Where can I take her?"

A sigh. "I'll send you an address. A safe house. She's better off there with protection until we sort this shit out. Is she all right?"

"Not sure. She'll need the clinic, what with having the baby and—"

"Go there, then. I'll send you that address instead."

The line went dead.

Pippa opened her eyes.

Nessa turned to her. "Are you okay with that?"

It had *sounded* like George on the phone but…

Pippa nodded and closed the door, hoping she hadn't jumped from the frying pan into the fire.

Chapter Six

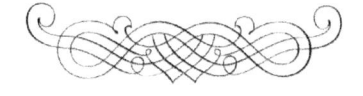

Crook sat in the drug flat a couple of doors down from his gaff and seethed, yet again, that Pippa still hadn't turned up. Another day had dawned, and he drank his extra-strong-shot coffee he'd had delivered. He'd had a late night, scouring the streets, hoping to find her on another patch, touting her wares. It was doing his nut in that she'd had the audacity to make a run for it—*and* that he couldn't find her. He'd asked so many people if they'd seen her that he'd lost count, and receiving answers in the negative had sent him to boiling point several times.

Where *was* she? And who the hell did she think she was to fuck off like that when she didn't have permission? She'd entered into a verbal contract with him and knew the score. She'd broken the rules, and he'd make sure she suffered for it.

Gopher, his main man, stood at the living room window, peering over at Kitchen Street, watching the girls at work through the telescope. The view from this floor was perfect, hence Crook renting here. He had a bird's-eye view and could keep track. All the girls knew—it kept them in line, wondering when he was observing them.

"How's it going out there?" he asked, the coffee finally hitting the spot.

"Fran's had a fair few punters already this morning, and it isn't even nine o'clock."

"The before-work crowd. Some like shags so it sets them up for the day. How many has she had?"

"Four."

Crook rubbed his hands together. "More money for me."

Gopher laughed. "They're all so dumb."

"What?"

"You know, paying you three quarters of their earnings."

"Good job I know what you mean, else I'd have been offended by you saying that. They're dumb for getting involved with me, yeah, but at the same time that means they're sensible, because if they didn't do as I say, didn't pay me, they'd be dead. But yeah, they're dumb to have fallen for my bullshit in the first place."

Crook had no intention of killing anyone, or hurting them, he didn't have the guts, but he'd never tell Gopher that. He'd cast aside his old name and life to become Crook, a face around here, someone women feared. Mind you, they didn't fear him until he'd shown his true colours. Prior to that, he was nice to them, roping them in, then, when he put them out to work on Kitchen, they were in his clutches so much they wouldn't dare go against him. He knew who their families were, knew their soft spots. One wrong move on their part, and they were toast—or so they thought—although he hadn't had to kill anyone yet. That would hopefully never happen. He didn't think he was quite ready for that level of violence yet, although he made out he was.

"Good job Fran's raking it in," Crook said. "It makes up what I'm losing now Pippa's not out there."

She'd been one of his highest earners before she'd hopped it, working all the hours to get herself out of the debt she owed him. Not only did he take a load of her wages, she also had to hand over one hundred nicker a day to pay back the loan he'd given her. She'd been in hock up to her eyeballs when he'd met her, and it had been so easy to ensnare her because she'd been desperate. She hadn't finished repaying it, so he was a few grand down. Maybe he'd take a fiver extra off each girl every evening so *they* covered Pippa's loan. Why should *he* go without because some slag had upped sticks?

He downed the rest of his coffee. Walked over to the window and took the telescope from Gopher. Instead of observing his own girls, he settled on those at Debbie's Corner a couple of streets away. They all dressed nice and didn't look skanky like his lot—he'd have to have a word with them about that. Debbie's were a cut above, that was obvious, and it annoyed him that business was brisker there than on Kitchen. She had even more girls in a parlour at the back of The Angel, slappers who charged a fair whack for men to fuck them on massage tables. He used to go in that pub a lot a year or two ago, plus he'd sampled some tarts from the corner to get some tips on how to run his own women. Sick of being poor, working at a factory, he'd branched out by himself. Best move he'd ever made, although every day he ran the risk of The Brothers finding out.

"Come on, let's go and pay Pippa's drug pushers a visit." He popped the telescope on the windowsill and went over to pick up his jacket. Shrugged it on and checked his gun was in the front pocket—one he only used to threaten.

Gopher gawped at him. "I thought you said we weren't going to do that. Messing with Dickie Feathers' family an' all that."

"But he's dead, and none of his mates are around to tell us to fuck off, are they. As for his bit of stuff and that kid of his—Chesney, isn't it?—what are they going to do, ring the pigs on us?"

They laughed at the absurdity of that, and Crook followed Gopher out of the flat. Crook drove to the 'office', knowing the way because they'd tailed Pippa there one night to see where she bought her gear from. The fact she hadn't been hooked on coke before Crook had met her and that *he'd* got her desperate for the high didn't concern him. He didn't experience one second of guilt for pulling her into his web. She was a money-maker to him, nothing more.

"Someone's here." Gopher parked beside another car.

"Dickie's bit on the side." Crook got out and approached the office door. The blinds, drawn on the door and the open window, meant he couldn't see jack shit, so he moved across to the pane on the right where one of the slats didn't quite meet. He peered through the slim gap, shading his eyes with his hand. "Oh, fuck me. Come and get an eyeful of this."

Gopher came over and took Crook's place. "Jesus, the state of her face."

Crook budged him out of the way. "Looks like she's been burnt."

Gopher pulled his gloves on and checked the door. It opened, and he pushed it inwards and stepped inside. Crook went in behind him, thinking he'd get the woman to hand over cash and drugs, seeing as she wasn't in any fit state to fight him off.

Marlborough, sitting on the floor, stared at them and shrank back as though they were monsters. "Did *she* send you?"

"Who's she?" Crook asked. Had there been a family spat? Had Nessa come round and had a go?

Marlborough swallowed, wincing at the pain that must have spread over her face at the movement. She contemplated for a second or two, maybe deciding whether she should tell them who she'd meant. "Doesn't matter."

"Oh, I think it does." Gopher kicked her in the side.

She cried out, and yellowish liquid seeped from a burn blister that had just popped on her cheek. "Leave me alone." She sounded tired. Defeated.

"Where are the drugs and cash?" Crook asked.

"We don't keep any here until the evenings," she said.

"Liar."

"It's true." She sighed. "I can't even be bothered to argue with you. Believe me or not, I don't care. Raid this place, and I still won't care. But I *can* tell you, when I get my hands on that bitch…"

"What bitch?" Crook pressed—she could be on about Pippa, and wouldn't that be a turn-up for the books?

"The one who burnt my fucking *face*!" Marlborough snapped.

Crook's temper gathered momentum. She was getting right on his nellies being disrespectful like that. "I gathered that, but *who* is she?"

Marlborough smiled snidely then winced again. "Like I'm going to tell *you*. I'd be in more shit than you can imagine if I said who did it. Is that why you're here? Mucking about pretending you don't know anything, when really, you do?"

How thick *was* she? By saying that, she'd let him know who the 'bitch' was. It didn't take much to work out it could be who he was after.

"Pippa," he said. "When was the last time she bought drugs off you?"

"I can't remember when she last *bought* them, but she was here a few days ago trying to get some on tick. I said no and sent her on her way."

Crook tried his usual trick to get people to talk. "You're lying."

"Just get out," she said. "I'm not lying, she *didn't* buy any, and she *did* ask for us to sub her some heroin."

Heroin? What the fuck?

"I'm not a charity," Marlborough rambled on, "so she can sod off if she thinks we do freebies. Why are you so bothered about her anyway?"

"She's missing. Owes me a wad of cash."

"Not my problem."

The way she'd said that…it got right under Crook's skin. He slid gloves on—fucked if he was touching her gammy face—and launched a right hook, so unlike him he stilled for a moment in surprise. His fist landed on her nose, and she flew backwards, whacking her head on the wall on her way down to the floor.

Gopher laughed his guts up and stared at her. "You've knocked her out cold."

"She was pissing me off. We'll come back another time. Chesney won't be able to hold back. He'll spill the beans if we push him hard enough."

Crook walked out and got in the car, convinced Pippa had been here. Gopher all but threw himself in the passenger seat and whooped, slamming the door closed, overexcited from the violence. Crook drove off to Kitchen Street and stopped by the kerb to speak to one of his girls.

He pressed the button to lower the window. "Any news?"

She shook her head. "Nah. I went round her flat again last night and she's still not answering. No one's seen her for ages. The post's covering the mat inside—I looked through the letterbox."

"Good girl. Keep your eyes peeled."

Crook sped away, narrowly missing a man in a suit getting into his Kia.

Gopher whooped again. "You should have rammed into the cunt."

Crook chuckled.

Yeah, he should have, but he didn't have the bottle.

Chapter Seven

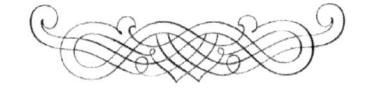

Chesney, in the same outfit as when he'd dropped the baby at St Matthew's, stopped his SUV outside the church. With no CCTV around here, he wasn't fussed about being clocked. If anyone reported him after he'd done his business, he'd make out he'd been to the shops up the road or something. Asif's Corner Store didn't have CCTV inside, the bloke too skinflint to bother getting any, saying he already paid the twins protection money, so that was enough of a deterrent. No one could dispute whether Chesney had been in there or not. If Asif said he hadn't, well, everyone knew he was getting on a bit and his mind wasn't all there, so who would believe him anyway?

Instead of what could go wrong, Chesney concentrated on the job ahead of him. What he'd seen on the local news last night had kept him awake, and he had to get this sorted before he went screwy. The stupid priest had mentioned a woman to the police, and everyone had been told to be on the lookout for her. Blonde, blue jeans, a hoody, around fifteen. While that was good because he hadn't said a *man*, at the same time it wasn't. Why mention a woman at all? It would have been better to stick to the original narrative that had been floating around the internet and on the telly—that Dublin had found the baby on the altar steps, no one else around.

How come things had changed? All right, Chesney had told Dublin not to tell anyone *he* had been there, but fucking Nora... Was he thick or what?

Hood pulled low, sunglasses on, Chesney stalked up to the church doors, one of them ajar. If anyone was inside, praying before work or whatever, he'd sit in a back pew and wait. Once people had left, he'd shut the door and, if Dublin wasn't around, he'd call out to him. Get him to lock them in so they could have a little 'chat'.

He stepped inside, relieved to find no parishioners or that nosy cow who helped Dublin out. Helen or whatever her name was. Hetty. Fuck, Hazel. The last thing he needed was that woman listening in. Chesney came here every Sunday with Mum so he'd had dealings with her, and his presence here as his normal self was why he'd had to put on an East End accent when speaking to the priest. Dublin would have recognised his real voice straight away, which wouldn't have been ideal.

The man himself knelt in front of the altar, head bowed.

"I need a word," Chesney shouted so his voice carried.

Dublin's head snapped up. "Oh God, it's you. Please, leave me alone."

"Can't do that. Are we alone?"
"Yes."

"Then get these doors locked. *Now.*"

Dublin rose and shuffled down the aisle as if he were an old man not a young one. Guilt bore down on him, that was obvious, and he didn't once glance at Chesney. Because he'd fucked up with the coppers? He took a bunch of keys out of his suit jacket pocket and inserted one in the lock. Turned it. Left the key there. Why, for ease of getting out should he want to escape? He went to sit on a nearby pew, acting as though his legs couldn't hold him up anymore.

"I know why you're here," Dublin said.

"What did you have to go and fuck things up for?" Chesney barked.

"Pardon?"

"I know it was you, so don't play innocent."

Dublin took a deep breath. "They came back yesterday, the police. Pushed me to answer questions. I had to come up with *something* to make them go away."

"No, what you had to do was stick to what you'd already said. Keep it simple. The less of a story you tell, the less you'll slip up."

"You weren't there. You don't know what it felt like to be pressured."

"I'll give you fucking pressured." Chesney stalked over to him and slapped him round the face. "You have *no idea* who you're messing with." He puffed his chest up, remembering when Dad had said that once, how scary and important he'd looked.

Dublin lifted a shaking hand to cradle his cheek. "They're searching for a woman, not a man. Isn't that a good thing?"

"Not really, because now they know you kept it from them all this time. It's been *days*. They'll be wondering what else you're keeping from them. They'll be back, I can fucking guarantee it."

"It's okay, I made sure the woman…the officer…I made sure she thought I was too upset the first time she spoke to me to remember much."

"And did she buy it?"

"Yes."

Chesney didn't believe him. This bloke was what Dad would have called a bastard liability, and something had to be done about him. Chesney had come here with that intention anyway, to shut him the fuck up. Tie off the loose end. Dublin being found dead would muddy the waters, send the police in another direction.

"Get in your office or whatever it's called."

Dublin's hand dropped to his lap, and he at last peered at Chesney, one side of his face going pale, the other streaked with a livid red handprint. "W-what?"

"You heard me. We're too close to the doors, get it? Someone might be outside, listening. You don't want your precious flock hearing what you've done, do you? Covering up for some kid who brought a dead baby here."

Dublin stood and swallowed. Glanced from the doors to Chesney.

"Don't bother. You won't get out in time." Chesney took a small gun out of the front pocket of his hoody. "Now *move* it."

Dublin whimpered like the pathetic prick he was and all but ran down the aisle. Chesney followed quickly—the twat might make for the door that led to the rear grounds. Catching up to him, Chesney gripped the priest's jacket collar and dug the barrel of the gun in his back.

"Nice and steady. No funny ideas."

Sniffling, Dublin led the way into a room with a desk, a chair, a battered fabric sofa, filing cabinets, and an ancient bureau—a bloody ugly wooden thing that must have been made when Mary and Joseph were around.

"Sit." Chesney shoved him towards the desk.

Dublin stumbled forward. He staggered to his seat and flopped into it, whimpering.

Chesney pointed the gun at him. "Where's the funeral money? It said on the news that people are donating for one, so you don't need that cash now."

Dublin shifted his wide-eyed gaze from the gun to somewhere beside him, then he dropped his attention to his lap. "The police have it."

"What?"

"They took it as evidence."

Chesney swallowed. He'd touched that money and the envelope without gloves on, so sure the priest would do as he'd said and pay for the funeral. Jesus Christ, he'd never been arrested before, so his prints weren't on file, but that didn't mean anything. If they caught up with him, somehow finding out he'd brought the baby here, they'd soon have proof it had been him. Or, if in future he got nicked for running the drug business with Mum, it would be flagged on the system that his prints matched those on file from *this* case.

Shitting hell.

"When you're out on a job, always wear gloves, son."

Chesney felt sick. He didn't even have any on *now*. Dad's warning had never seemed so frightening, such a portent of what could happen—him being arrested, sent down. He hadn't touched anything in the church today, so that was all right, and he came here with Mum anyway. There would be thousands of prints all over this place—but not in this room, so he'd better be careful.

His phone rang in his pocket, and he took it out to see who it was. Mum.

He ignored it and put the mobile away.

"Have you got any notes about this, a diary, on a computer?" Chesney blew out a long breath to steady himself. He'd almost spoken in his normal voice then, panic taking him out of the thug role and into his true self. "Any evidence that it was me?"

"No, I wouldn't be so stupid."

"But you were stupid enough to let the coppers take the money. What were you *playing* at?"

"You scared me. I was in a mess. I didn't even see them take it! I wasn't thinking straight."

You and me both, you godly bastard. "You'd better not be lying."

"I'm not! Please, I'm sorry for everything I've done, but… There's no need for the gun. I'm not going to say anything else to anyone."

"No, you're not."

Chesney pulled the trigger.

Had Dad felt like this when he'd shot someone? Where was the joy, the utter euphoria he'd told Chesney about? Where was the happy dance? To be honest, this was nothing but a damp squib, a total letdown. Maybe guilt at killing a man of the cloth had something to do with it. Dad didn't hold with 'all that religious bollocks', but Mum did, so Chesney had grown up with firm Christian teachings. It was laughable really, considering what he and Mum did to make a crust. Christian criminals who thought nothing of hurting people who fucked them about. Saying that, Dad had been the one to mete out punishments regarding their drug business until the day he'd died, so Chesney had only acted the hardman, a verbal prop for his old man. His first foray into standing in his dad's shoes had ended up with the baby dying, Dublin's brains spattered on the wall opposite, and later on today, Pippa's murder.

It hadn't gone too well, had it.

His phone rang again. Mum.

"Piss off," he mumbled and tutted, stuffing the gun in his pocket.

She'd only be telling him Nessa had arrived, so he didn't bother answering. Instead, he slid his mobile away and stared at Dublin to get some kind of 'I'm a Gangster' feeling, but nothing came, just dread at being caught for this *and* the baby.

Maybe, like Mum had said, he *wasn't* cut from the same cloth as Dickie Feathers. Maybe he *wasn't* the kind of man suited to this life, although he enjoyed the power he had over the druggies.

Having power sitting inside him was different to wielding it, though.

Out of morbid curiosity, he walked over and checked the back of Dublin's head. The exit wound had him recoiling, and he bumped into the side of a filing cabinet beside the desk, knocking something off. Whatever it was smashed on the floor. He turned to see what it was. A vase or maybe an urn, and amongst the cracked pieces, the envelope he'd handed to Dublin. Chesney snatched it up, relief coasting through him, and looked inside. Only about one hundred pounds left.

"You fucking thieving bastard."

If Dublin wasn't dead, he'd kill him all over again.

"You spent most of that money! What on?"

He shoved it in his hoody pocket and backed to the door, bumping into something else.

"For fuck's *sake*!"

He spun, coming face to face with that Hazel woman standing in the doorway. She must have come in via the back. So she had her own key, or had the door been open? Chesney cursed himself for not checking that. The old bat stared at him, eyes as round as her middle, permed hair wobbling with her indignation, and plonked her hands on her hips.

"What are you doing in there?" she demanded, seemingly unfazed that he had sunglasses on indoors.

Chesney took the gun out of his pocket, no hesitation. It was what Dad would have done. He aimed it at her, and she took a step backwards, hands up, registering that she'd walked in on something that was none of her fucking business. A quick glance into the room, and she screamed, clearly seeing Dublin for the first time.

"Oh my God. The father, what have you done? Oh my God…"

Chesney couldn't be arsed to explain. He shot her in the forehead. Her body flung backwards, hitting the wall of the little hallway, sinking down to the stone-flagged floor. The move smeared the blood and brains on the white paintwork, and she jerked, her fingers twitching, nerve endings firing for the last time. Chesney gawped at her, his chest tight with tension, still no 'I'm a Gangster' vibes going on.

He ran, out into the main body of the church and up the aisle. His hood pushed upwards from his speed, so he pulled it back down. His face broke out in sweat, the heat steaming up his sunglasses, and he took a second to put his gun away and breathe in the stillness. To centre himself. To get calm.

"It'll be all right, it'll be all right…"

Sleeve over his hand, he turned the key in the lock. What if someone stood outside on the steps, waiting to come in? He opened the door just enough to peer out. Then more. He poked his head round.

No one.

He went out, closing the door. Walked down the steps, appearing calmer than he felt, and got into his motor. Drove away, the seat belt alarm pinging. At the end of the street, he stopped outside Asif's and sorted the belt, then got going again.

The shakes gripped him two streets away. Hazel arriving on the scene hadn't been factored in, and while he didn't care she was dead, he *did* care that the search for the killer would be even bigger now because he'd done two people over. What else could he have done, though? If he'd let her live, she'd have given the police his description, and while that was the same as any number of lads in London, it took the focus off the coppers searching for a woman. It was obvious the two murders were related to the baby, wasn't it? Or would they think it was something else, seeing as Hazel hadn't been there when the kid had been handed over?

He couldn't think about that now. There was Pippa to deal with, and he wanted to watch how Nessa killed her, get some tips. Form a bond with his sister so they became a formidable team. Two feathers from the same man-bird, preening.

He arrived at the office, annoyed only Mum's car was there. Where was Nessa? Had she got shitfaced at Dad's wake and currently slept it off? What time had Mum told her to be here anyway? Chesney had assumed it would be early, but maybe they'd planned it for later on.

It pissed him off being left out of the loop.

Annoyed, especially because he felt nothing but worry over killing Dublin and Hazel now he'd had time to think about his actions, he tried to slide his key into the office door and frowned. Mum must have left her key on the inside; the door was unlocked. He pushed it inwards, his attention going straight to the radiator, but Pippa wasn't there. For fuck's sake, had Nessa killed her already? He swung his gaze to the desk on the left. No Mum.

He stepped inside.

Mum lay on the floor. Blood oozed from a couple of gashes on the side of her head. Time stalled, and Chesney, suspended in a moment of disbelief, could do nothing but stare. His heart rate sped up, and he blinked away the fog in his brain. Mum's *face*... The skin appeared to have been boiled, the top layers no longer there, meaty flesh taking its place. Her phone, half in one limp hand, half on the floor, had a dark screen. She'd tried to phone him twice, and he'd ignored her.

Shit.

Why was she out of it?

He rushed over and, down on his knees, checked for a pulse. It throbbed steadily, so that was something. Had she passed out from the pain?

With no Pippa here, did that mean she'd attacked Mum? Or had Nessa arrived and done it, taking Pippa with her? Chesney had questioned Mum's idea of bringing his sister into the equation, they didn't know much about her other than what Dad had told them, but they'd assumed Nessa was kosher.

Chesney plopped down on his backside, not knowing what to do. If he took Mum to a hospital, they'd ask too many questions. The police would be brought in for an attack like this. The forensic lot would be called, and they'd go over the office—and find evidence that Pippa had been here. And the residue of drugs.

"Mum. Mum? Wake up. I don't know what to do."

Mum slept on.
Chesney cried.

Chapter Eight

Usually, on a Monday after work, Pippa went home and microwaved one of the meals she'd taken out of the freezer that morning (she batch cooked on Sundays). Yet here she was, in the Old Woodshed, sitting at a table in the corner with Fiona, Theresa, and Lillibet. She'd felt uncomfortable at first, but once the first vodka had gone down, she'd loosened up.

Especially as the trio were so nice to her, apologising for never inviting her out before now.

"We thought you were like Stephanie," Theresa said, her face contorted into a spiteful expression. "I mean, she's so horrible."

"I didn't think she was," Pippa said, "not until she turned funny on me anyway."

"But you stood up for yourself and gave as good as you got," Lillibet said. "If you give her an inch she'll take a yard, trust me on that. People like her need to be kept at arm's length. To be honest, that's the real reason we didn't get involved with you. Once burned an' all that."

Pippa had only been working at Ford and Sons for six months. "Did something happen before I came along, then?"

Fiona took a deep breath. "You could say that."

Pippa sipped more of her drink, bravery paying her a visit enough for her to ask, "What was it?"

"We did let her into our circle, but it went wrong." Fiona glanced at her friends as if asking for permission to share. It seemed they'd given it, because she said, "Okay, so we thought she was the same as us, where she liked getting pissed at the weekends and copping off with men. Don't get me wrong, we're not slags or anything, but if a bloke happens to come along, why

not? But she spent the whole night berating us, making out we were deviants or something. Fucking hell, you'd think we had to be nuns. She even went so far as to say God would frown on us, and that was it for me. I told her to fuck off, and she left."

"How was it at work after that?" Pippa asked.

"Well, seems she's not as Christian as she likes to make out," Lillibet said. "She started fucking about with our files, like she did to you today, and over the space of a week, all of us were called in to Mr Ford's office to be asked what we were playing at."

"She's a nutbag," Theresa said. "Completely off her rocker."

"Don't forget the emails," Lillibet said.

Fiona rolled her eyes. "Shit, yes."

"What about them?" Pippa asked.

"We kept getting ones from prospective clients. They'd been sent overnight, there in the inbox when we started work for the day. Just the usual enquiries at first, then when we'd answered all the questions they asked, they provided a phone number and told us to call them. I swear to God, it shit me up when I rang it."

Pippa tensed. "What happened?"

"It was a mobile number. I got a recorded message."

"We all had the same thing happen," Fiona said.

Lillibet continued. "It said something like, 'Slappers are the work of the Devil. Repent or go to Hell for your sins.' But it was this weird voice, it'd been changed by electronics or something. Then it laughed." She shuddered.

Theresa fiddled with the ruby pendant on her necklace. "I'm all for a laugh and whatever, but that wasn't funny. Lillibet told us about it at lunch, then in the afternoon, I rang my client and got the same message. By then, even though it had shit us up, we worked out it had to be Stephanie. Don't ask me how, we just knew. Maybe it was the Devil angle, the sins thing. So an hour later, Fiona had to ring a 'client', and she got the message. Me and Lillibet were watching Stephanie at the time, and she was staring over at Fiona as if she wanted to see her reaction. She caught us looking and smirked like she always does."

"So what did you do?"

"We came here after work and chatted about it. Thought of ways to get her back. We ended up freezing her out and only talking to her if we had to for work."

Fiona sighed. "Honestly, she's not right in the head, so be careful. If you get new client emails tomorrow, and they ask a lot of questions, then she's playing the same game with you."

Pippa digested that. "But if she's all God-loving and whatnot, why be so mean?"

"Who the hell knows," Fiona said. "Now we're basically one hundred percent it's her being a cow, we should do something about it."

"Like what?" A warm glow spread inside Pippa at being included in this.

"We'll fuck her over," Theresa said, sounding sinister. "Big time."

No weird emails had come from prospective clients, just regular ones. The credit card had arrived early on Friday with a four grand limit. Pippa had never been so excited. On Saturday morning, she visited the charity shop and bought lots of clothes and shoes, snagging a Gucci handbag for a steal. Now she'd had time to get to know them a little, she didn't think her new friends were that bothered about what she looked like, they were nice to her, but for her own sense of self-worth, she wanted to be like them.

At ten to eight, she got a taxi to The Bar and stood outside for a moment to get her bearings. She hadn't been there before and wanted to check whether she'd be safe. A line of cabs snaked around the rank, ready to take people to the clubs a mile or so away, and people queued at a kebab van. Down the street, every other place was a pub, the pavements packed with smokers. She'd be all right.

She pushed open the door to The Bar and walked inside, nervous. It had been one thing to go with the girls to the Old Woodshed after work on Monday because they'd all gone there together, but this was her first time meeting them outside of that setting. What if they didn't show? What would she do then? How would she feel?

Relief swam through her. They stood at the bar, ordering drinks. Pippa went up to them and, far from feeling like the outsider, she honestly thought she belonged. They squealed and hugged her, and, crushed inside a four-way embrace, she fought back tears. So this was what she'd been missing? This sense of inclusion?

They had two drinks in The Bar then moved on to the next pub. The Wheatsheaf, modern with mood lighting, had a disco on. Buoyed up by two shots of vodka, Pippa tapped her foot to the music, self-consciousness seeping away with every minute that passed. Theresa sang loudly, waving her glass about, and Lillibet chatted to some bloke. Fiona eyed up another fella, so Pippa gravitated to Theresa, and they danced for a bit.

In the next pub down the line, Cuban Cocktails, they shared a jug of Red Dragon, whatever that was. Pippa reckoned it had gin and orange juice in it, but as for the rest, she had no idea. And she didn't care. She needed the booze to allow her to do what they'd planned before they headed to a club, The Roxy.

They piled into a taxi which took them to the next street along from Stephanie's. It parked outside another pub, The Lion. Fiona had explained that they didn't want to get caught for what they were about to do, obviously, and they needed an alibi. As The Lion was notorious for pissheads who didn't know their arse from their elbow, no one except the bar staff would notice they'd nipped out, and it was that busy, Pippa didn't think they'd even spot them leaving.

One more drink, and they set off, keeping to the shadows. Pippa sobered up a tad, the hilarity of the night ebbing away at the thought of what was to come. While she detested Stephanie for being rude to her and wanting to get her in trouble with Mr Ford, **and** *for being so weird to the others with those emails and recorded phone messages, it still didn't sit right.*

Stephanie lived in a quiet street of Victorian homes. Many of the houses appeared to be sectioned off into flats. With no one around, Fiona led the way down an alley between two houses and, putting gloves on out of her pocket, she opened a side gate. She walked through, everyone else following. Pippa, at the rear, had an ominous feeling and wanted to bolt, but instead she closed the gate with her elbow and tailed the others to a back door. Fiona knocked on it. A light snapped on inside, glowing around the Venetian blind over the door glass.

Two of the slats parted, piggy eyes filling the gap.

"Here she is, girls," Fiona whispered. "Get your bloody gloves on."

The door opened, and Stephanie filled the frame. "What do you lot want? And how did you know where I live?"

Fiona took charge. "I followed you once, all right?"

"Not too creepy, then," Stephanie retorted. "Like I said, what do you want?"

Fiona's hands shot out, and she gave their colleague a big shove to the chest. Stephanie staggered backwards, and Fiona entered the house. Theresa went next, then Lillibet, and Pippa hung back, still outside as her new friends crowded around Stephanie who'd plastered her back to the far wall.

"Shut the door," Fiona said.

Fuck it.

Pippa put her gloves on, stepped inside, and did as she'd been asked, shaking a little. To see what amounted to a pack of wolves surrounding their prey wasn't as funny as she'd imagined. Fiona hit Stephanie first, her tight fist smacking into her nose. Stephanie let out a cry of alarm, her hand going up to the offended spot.

"What was that for?" Stephanie whined.

"You know what it's for." Theresa launched a right hook into their enemy's stomach. "You fucked over the wrong people, lady."

Pippa almost laughed at that. Theresa had sounded so silly.

"The bodging of our work," Theresa went on with another gut punch. "Those emails." Punch. "Those stupid voicemail messages." Punch.

"What?" Stephanie said.

"Don't make out you're innocent," Fiona snarled. "And if you tell anyone about this, you're going to look stupid because no one would believe we'd do it."

Stephanie sank to the floor, clutching her belly. She groaned, her head bent. Lillibet did a swinging side kick, the toe of her stiletto smacking into Stephanie's temple. The woman slowly slid onto her side, covering her head with her hands. It seemed to go by in a blur after that, lots of kicks and thumps, until Stephanie couldn't shield herself any longer, her arms dropping.

"Get a kick in, then!" Fiona said to Pippa.

Oh God. Oh God…

Pippa swallowed and went over there, striking Stephanie in the ribs rather than her head. Fiona had no such reservations, and her foot landed on the face, sending Stephanie's head back to whack into the wall. Puffy, bruised eyes closed, Stephanie lay still, her chest rising and falling shallowly. Pippa backed away to the door and wrenched it open, nauseated, desperate for fresh air. Her friends joined her, and Fiona switched the light off then closed the door.

"What if she grasses us up?" Pippa whispered, fear paving a path through her.

"Then like we agreed, we deny it," Fiona said. "Come on, gloves off. Back to The Lion."

They traipsed to the pub, Pippa paranoid all the way that someone had seen them. Inside, she drank a double vodka straight back and ordered another. They veered away from the bar to sit in a corner, the others happily chair dancing and laughing. Pippa made a show of joining in, but she wasn't feeling it.

What if Stephanie phoned the police?

Chapter Nine

At the clinic on The Moon Estate, George paced the corridor outside the room Pippa was being examined in. Greg sat on one of the comfy visitor chairs beside Nessa who whittled her fingers and looked pale as eff. As always, no staff had questioned them about Pippa except to ask what she needed help with. The 'why' didn't matter—they were paid hefty sums to keep their gobs shut, even if it *did* involve the baby left in the church.

"Tell me what the fuck's going on," George said.

Nessa sighed. "Yesterday, at the crematorium, Dad's bit of stuff spoke to me. Said they run a drug business out of an office and Pippa had come for some gear. There'd been an argument or something, and Chesney, the mistress' son who happens to be my half-brother, had pushed Pippa. She landed on the floor, and it set off her labour. Turns out she gave birth and Chesney dumped the baby."

George scowled. "Yesterday. And you're just telling us this today."

"I wanted to see what was what before I let you know. For all I knew, it was all a load of bullshit, a way to get me to work for their 'family' business, lure me there. Marlborough, that's Dickie's bit on the side, said they needed me to take his place. I'd never heard of him running a drug shop so didn't believe her, hence my plan to visit it today *then* tell you. Plus, if it was true, I wanted to get Pippa out of there because Marlborough asked me to kill her."

George didn't like the idea of some woman ordering another about like that, especially if it involved murder. Who the fuck did that Marlborough bint think she was? "You what?"

"I know…"

"And how were you going to do *that*?"

"I don't know, maybe say I like to kill in private or something so I could get away with not doing it in front of them. Make out I'd take some pictures of her dead so they had proof, get the poor cow to pose as if she'd snuffed it. I was just bothered about saving her more than anything. How I'd do that and convince them I was on the level, I wasn't sure. I was going to wing it."

He believed her but looked at Greg to check if his twin felt the same. Seemed he did. Greg shook his head, likely at Marlborough's audacity, gadding around like some gangster moll. George had never liked Dickie, hence them sacking him when they'd taken over Cardigan. For one, he'd been too old to be of much use, and two, Dickie had a habit of putting his nose where it didn't belong, and it had pissed George off. He hadn't known the bloke had a bit on the side, though, *and* they'd had a son.

He stopped pacing and leaned on the wall. "Fair enough, I can see why you'd go down that route, but next time, if you hear anything, tell us straight away, whether you think it's bollocks or not. If you had, Pippa would be saved by now because we'd have collected her while the office was empty. Instead, she spent another night at risk."

"She wouldn't have been at risk. Marlborough and Chesney held a different wake for Dickie at the Crosshatch Arms and they'd have been bladdered."

"But what if Chesney got so pissed up he went to the office and killed her?"

"I didn't think of that."

"No, you didn't." George reined his temper in. *What's done is done.* "The baby was found *days* ago. Why had they kept Pippa that long?"

Nessa shrugged. "Probably working out what to do with her as well as coping with Dickie being dead. I don't know."

"So what happened this morning?"

"I was on my way to their office. Saw a woman running. Stopped and asked if she was okay. I gathered it was her straight off so didn't want her getting away. I needed her kept safe, away from Marlborough and Chesney."

"Okay, here's what we're going to do. You're going to go to the office in a bit, turn up as if you're there to kill Pippa. When they tell you what went on, big it up that Pippa will likely have come to see us for help or would have gone to the police so they'll need to lie low for a bit. I want those two in a specific location, the safe house I mentioned on the phone—I can't be bothered with stalking them and picking them up, I'm not in the mood for that sort of malarky. Say it's Dickie's bolthole or something. We'll collect them from there."

A middle-aged, black-haired doctor came out of the room, cutting off the conversation. He kept himself trim and had a James Bond air about him, all debonair and good with the ladies.

"Everything all right?" George asked.

"As well as she can be in the circumstances. I'll prescribe antibiotics in case of infection—she hasn't been able to bathe or shower, and after giving birth, well…"

George didn't need to know the ins and outs of that. "Is she okay to leave?"

"Yes, providing she gets help for her addiction."

"Which is?"

"Cocaine and alcohol, although she said the man gave her what she thinks is heroin to keep her quiet. We can do blood tests if you like, see what's in her system."

"Nah, she's likely right."

"Will you put her into rehab, or do you require me to give you the details of a place she can go?"

"It's discreet?"

"As discreet as we are, otherwise I wouldn't have suggested it."

George didn't like his tone but let it go. "Yeah, get me the address. Could you organise a room for her there?"

"Of course, but it will cost you. I itemise my bills down to the smallest thing, even as much as making a phone call."

"I didn't expect anything less." *Fucking greedy cunt.*

The doctor walked off down the hall, his shoes squeaking against the shiny lino. He disappeared through another doorway, no doubt to make that phone call and add one hundred nicker to the bill.

"You go in first," George said to Nessa. "I don't need her crapping her pants seeing us two barging in."

Nessa got up and entered the room.

George sat beside Greg, his stomach in knots. "A baby. He killed a *baby*."

"Hmm. Then there's the drugs. How did we not know about this?"

George sighed. "The same as we didn't know about the other den we discovered in that flat ages ago. People are clever, and the druggies won't grass on their suppliers." He stood. "Come on. Let's go and see what she has to say for herself."

George led the way. He strode inside, trying to make himself appear smaller, less imposing. He didn't want to scare Pippa into a mute. It was clear she hadn't washed in days, her hair greasy and skin sallow. She stared at him, her eyes going wide, and reached out for Nessa's hand, probably seeing her as an ally, even though they hadn't known each other five minutes. George sat on a chair next to the bed, and Greg remained by the closed door.

"Listen, love," George said. "You're not in the shit, all right? We're going to help you.

Marlborough and Chesney will be dealt with for what they've done to you."

Pippa chuffed out a laugh. "You can't help me. Crook won't be happy about this. He'll beat the crap out of me when I go back home."

"Who the fuck is Crook?"

"My pimp."

George's blood all but boiled. "Was the baby…?"

Pippa winced. "Not his, no. He belongs to a man who refused to wear a condom. That's me putting it politely."

"He raped you?"

Pippa nodded.

George stood. Paced again. When he got hold of that piece of scum, he'd fucking do him. "Do you know who he is?"

"Crook's right-hand man. Gopher. Not his real name."

"Obviously."

"They've both got flats in Orange Street. Crook is number fifty, Gopher next door at fifty-one. Crook also rents fifty-two, which is where he runs the business from."

"Then we'll find them, kill them an' all. Where are you based when you work?"

"On Kitchen Street. It's like Debbie's Corner. From his flat, he can see us all working—or not. Spies on us with a telescope."

George glanced at Greg, speaking without words: *None of the residents have said about this, nor has Len in the corner shop on Kitchen. He needs a serious lesson.*

Greg nodded.

George returned his attention to Pippa. "Do you want to get clean? I mean the drugs."

"Of course I do. Crook forced me to take them. To keep me needing more, needing *him*. I didn't even want to be a sex worker. He...he persuaded me. I needed money, I..."

"Life sends us down the wrong road sometimes. Don't beat yourself up over it. You're going to rehab. You'll be safe there. One of our men, Will, he'll take you, stay with you. I'll arrange that with the doctor here so those at the rehab place don't kick up a stink." He gave her Will's description. "I'll give him a code word to say when he picks you up so you know it's definitely him, all right? Actually, hold on..." He took his phone out and rang Will on a video chat. Explained things. Swung the screen round so

Pippa could see who he was. Call ended, George let out a long breath. "You okay with all that?"

"Yes. Thank you. I… My baby…"

"When his body is released—shit, sorry, that was a bit blunt. When he's allowed to be buried, we'll take you to the funeral. The police will likely be there to see if you turn up, so as far as anyone's concerned, you're just another mourner. A lot of strangers will be there, seems like the whole of London loves your little boy, so maybe no one will take any notice of you."

"Will the rehab place let me go?"

George laughed. "*Let* you? They'll do whatever we fucking say, sweetheart. That's how it works in our world. They're paid to do as they're told."

A phone rang.

Nessa appeared confused for a second then pulled a mobile from her pocket. "They gave me a burner. I didn't recognise the ringtone."

"Put it on speaker," Greg said.

Nessa did that, then, "Hello?"

"Where are you?" a posh male asked.

"In my flat, why?"

"Mum's…that *bitch* attacked my mum! She's all burnt and shit."

George hadn't had a chance to ask Pippa how she'd escaped, but he laughed inside at the 'burnt' comment.

"What?" Nessa screeched, in actor mode. "Have you taken her to a hospital?"

"No. I've been sitting on the floor with her for ages. She won't wake up."

"Christ, Chesney. Have you at least put cold wet cloths on her face to take the heat out?"

"I didn't know that's what you're meant to do."

"Bloody hell! Her skin will have kept cooking."

"Oh God…"

"Where's the druggy?" Nessa gave Pippa an apologetic look.

"Fucked off somewhere. That's the last thing I need, that Crook prick coming here and giving me grief, and you can bet that's where she's gone."

"Wait for me. I'll be there in a bit. We'll sort something out between us."

"Cheers, sis."

Nessa cringed and cut the call. "Sis. I bloody *hate* him calling me that."

George cocked his head at Pippa. "So you burnt her, did you?"

Pippa smiled. "With boiled water from the kettle."

"Good girl. Right, we'll wait here with you until Will arrives. You can have a shower and put on some of the clothes the clinic keeps for situations like this. They'll probably have some slippers hanging about. Nessa, off you go and do your thing. Keep us updated. I'll send you the location address of where to take them."

Nessa stood and gazed down at Pippa. "Take care, love."

"Thank you," Pippa said. "For everything."

Nessa walked out, tears in her eyes.

"Soft tart," George muttered, a bit emotional himself.

Chapter Ten

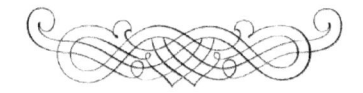

Janine hadn't expected to visit the church just yet to question Dublin again today, but she'd been called out to what could only be described as a pair of execution killings. A shot to the forehead of each victim spoke of quick murders to shut Dublin and the woman up. Regarding little Luke? Had the mystery teenage girl done this?

It wasn't unheard of for teenagers to kill, especially not in London. There was too much of this shit going on for her liking, kids acting like adults, roped into belonging to gangs, or they were just plain nasty people who thought nothing of taking a life. Just last week Janine had walked past the booking desk in the custody suite and caught the tail end of some lad bragging that he'd made his first kill, as if it was something to be proud of.

He was twelve. *Twelve*.

She sighed into her mask and moved to stand near the dead woman in a narrow passageway, full protectives on, Colin beside her.

"Anyone found out who she is yet?" she called out, frustrated with waiting.

PC Doddy rushed over from where he stood by the altar with the lady who'd found the bodies. "The witness said she's called Hazel Jones. She was sixty last week, had a big party and everything. She worked at the Crosshatch, a chef, and helped the father out."

"Cheers."

Janine studied Hazel. Sixty? She looked a decade older, her clothing like the trends of the eighties, although saying that, the pleated skirts had recently been back in fashion, as had the puffed-sleeve flowery blouses with frills all over the place. Not something Janine would wear; she'd walked past them in horror while in Primark. They'd reminded her too much of her mother.

She'd seen enough gunshot wounds to know the bullet had struck at close range; Jim would likely confirm it when he arrived. She went through the options. One, the killer had seen to Dublin first, was perhaps leaving the office, and had been confronted with Hazel. Or two, he could have been walking towards the office, seen Hazel, backed into the doorway, then killed her, turning afterwards to blast Dublin.

Or *was* it a she, the teenage girl who'd given birth to Luke?

She put her thoughts to Colin.

"Dunno," he said. "It might not even be related to that. Dublin said people have been coming here to nick money out of the donation box, remember. It could be something like that, a coincidence."

"I suppose so."

Janine stepped past Hazel, careful to mind the blood spatter on the floor, even though the photos had already been taken, and stood in the office doorway. Dublin sat in his desk chair, so did that mean he'd known his killer or had at least been comfortable in their presence? A vase of some kind had been smashed, which could indicate a tussle, where the killer had manhandled the priest towards the desk and knocked it off when shoving him into the seat. Blood marred the wall behind the body. The back of the chair wasn't to head height, it reached his shoulders, so the bullet had embedded in the wall, the centrepiece to dark, drying blood on the paintwork. She turned to check the passageway and found the same thing there, the spent casing on the floor beside Hazel. She looked for the other one and spotted it on the office floor.

"Whoever it was didn't think to take the casings," she said. "Nor did they dig the bullets out of the walls, so either they're not intending to use that gun again, they were rushed and had to get out, or they don't give a shit what they left behind."

"Let's hope the bullet striations match something in our files." Colin sniffed. "Then again, if that gun was used in a previous crime which hasn't been solved, we're up shit creek on that score."

Janine nodded. "Sod hanging around waiting for Jim, it's obvious what happened here. We'll go and speak to the lady who found them."

In the passageway, Janine and Colin stripped out of their protectives, popped them in the designated bags, and put on fresh gloves and booties to go into the main part of the church. The lady in question stood in front of the altar steps, also in booties, with PC Doddy. About forty, with long blonde hair, she had a black suit on as if she'd been on her way to work and had nipped to the church first. A red blouse, no frills in sight.

Janine smiled and approached her. "I'm Detective Inspector Janine Sheldon, and this is my partner, Colin Broadly. I know you've also spoken to PC Doddy, but I'm afraid we're going to have to chat to you, too. I appreciate it's hard, you've had a shock, but the sooner we can get any information the better. I'll record the interview. It'll save you making another statement later on."

"Okay."

"What's your name first?"

"Korinne Cummings."

"Thanks." Janine set up the recording, said what she had to say for the tape, then dived in. "Can you tell me what happened? Start from before you entered the church."

"I parked out the front behind a light-blue Transit, or was it grey? I think it was an Amazon Prime one anyway. I was coming here to speak to Father Dublin about donating some things for the foodbank he runs. My daughter works for Co-op, and they have a lot of stuff going begging at the end of the day. It's fresh produce, so I wasn't sure if the father took that kind of thing. I came in and called out to him. He didn't come to see me, which is odd, as he's usually on his way as soon as the door creaks, so I walked down the passageway and…and I saw Hazel."

Janine smiled to encourage her to continue.

Korinne fiddled with her chin, pinching it. "She…she was dead, and I screamed. I rang the police and—"

"Using your phone or the one in the office?"

"Mine. The man on the other end asked me if anyone else was there. I poked my head round the office door and… Oh God, hang on a minute, I can't…can't…"

Korinne took a few deep breaths. Janine waited—she'd like to say patiently, but she wasn't bloody patient at all. She wanted all the answers *now*.

"…and I saw Father Dublin. I told the man what I was looking at, and he said to get out in case the killer was still here. I went to the front steps, shitting myself, and then the police came. Really quick, they were. They took my shoes and fingerprints."

"That will be to eliminate you. You trod in blood, I expect. Forensics will check the shoes to make sure there aren't any tell-tale spatters on them."

Korinne reared her head back, eyes wide. "What, as if *I* killed them?"

"We have to be sure."

"But it wasn't *me*. I swear it wasn't."

"I don't think it was, but like I said, we have to be sure. Before you came into the church, did you see anyone hanging around?"

"Not hanging around, no, but there was a woman with a pushchair, going towards Asif's."

"Asif's?"

"The corner shop up the end there."

"What did she look like?"

"Blonde hair in a bun. Taller than me. Skinny. Twenty-odd."

"And when you came out to wait for the officers? What about then?"

Korinne shook her head while thinking, as though that would knock her memories loose enough for her to pluck them up and repeat them. "Um, a man, he had a grey suit on. An umbrella used as a cane. He was waiting outside Cobblers, you know, the shop where you get your soles replaced. I'd say he was seventyish."

"Okay. Anyone else?"

"Someone in their car. On their phone. They were looking at it, not speaking into it. I couldn't see if it was a man or a woman because I only saw the hands holding the phone in front of the steering wheel."

The killer reporting in that the job had been done? "What car was it?"

"A blue Volvo, I don't know what kind."

"What sort of blue?"

"Dark. Navy."

"Did you note the number plate?"

"No."

"And was that all? You didn't see anyone else?"

"I was too busy leaning on the porch wall, trying to stop shaking. It all hit me, what I'd seen, and I couldn't stop crying."

"Thanks, you've been very helpful. Is there someone who can come and collect you?"

"I've got my car outside."

Janine raised her eyebrows. "So you'll drive with no shoes on?"

Korinne stared down at her bootied feet. "Oh."

Janine looked at the PC. "Can you arrange for Korinne to get home, please?"

"Will do."

"And pass on those descriptions to whoever arrives to do door-to-door enquiries."

Janine signed the recording off, saved it, and wandered down the aisle, Colin trailing behind her. At the doors, she noted a key in the lock. Why hadn't the killer secured the door after they'd left, giving them more time to get away before the bodies were discovered? Or were they in such a panic that they hadn't been thinking rationally?

She phoned in to arrange for more officers to canvas the street. Maybe someone along here had seen the woman with the buggy, the man holding an umbrella, the Volvo owner, and the Amazon person. Then she rang one of the DCs on her team to action them to search up navy Volvos and contact Amazon to see which drivers had been in the street this morning. Also, to find the next of kins for Hazel and Dublin.

She slid her phone away. "We'll speak to the NOKs once their details come back and after we've seen Asif. Who knows, we might get lucky and the killer popped into his shop."

If Asif didn't talk—or *wouldn't* talk—she knew two brick shithouses who could make him.

Let's hope it doesn't come to that.

Asif had been more than happy to provide fuck all information, although Janine believed he genuinely didn't know anything. Dublin's family lived in Sheffield, so the death knock had been passed to South Yorkshire Police, but Hazel had lived around the corner with her husband, who, as expected, hadn't taken the news well. He'd collapsed, and Colin had phoned for an ambulance. A suspected heart attack.

On their walk back to the church, Janine's burner phone buzzed in her pocket.

Fuck it. What do the twins want?

She stopped outside a poky café. "Why don't you go in there and fill your guts with bacon rolls or something, Col. I need a moment to take this phone call."

Colin ambled off, smiling, and Janine took her mobile out of her pocket. She clocked her bodyguard boyfriend over the road, watching her. Swiped her screen.

"I'm at a scene," she said, moving to stand in the doorway of an empty shop.

"Boo-hoo." George.

She sighed at his lack of sympathy. "What do you want?"

"We know who killed the baby."

Her stomach danced with butterflies. "*What?*"

"You heard me. We're dealing with them ourselves for reasons I can't be arsed to go into at the minute."

"Fucking *hell*, George! This one's got right under my skin, and *I* want the collar." She paused. "Hang on, you said *them*."

"One killer, one accomplice. Mother and son."

"Christ. What was it, a teenage pregnancy and the father of the baby and his mum forced an illegal abortion on her or tried to do it themselves?"

"Nope. She isn't a teen."

Janine waited for an explanation. With nothing forthcoming, she gathered George was in one of his awkward moods. "Listen, you. I'm not playing games today. This case is fucking horrible, and now the priest and a woman have been shot at the church where Luke was found."

"Luke?"

"The baby."

"Right, so you think they were killed by the baby's murderer?"

"Don't you?"

"It's likely."

Janine tapped her foot. "Fine, if you're going after them, I at least want their bodies and proof it was them left somewhere for us to find, like you've done before. I need a proper link between them and the mother, meaning the mum's blood on them, so prick her finger or something, whatever you need to do. There's also the matter of the gun used to kill the priest and a lady called Hazel. Get it for me. I can't let this one go without some kind of justice. The public are going mental over Luke's death, and God knows what they'll make of today's murders, so we can't afford for the killers to disappear in the Thames in your usual manner."

George must have covered the mouthpiece as muffled sounds came down the line. Janine's patience had been thin before, but right this second, she wanted to scream.

"George?" she barked.

The line cleared. "Not a problem. You'll have them by tonight."

"Why not now?"

"Because I'm sending a mole in to get them to a specific location."

She rolled her eyes. "A mole? Christ, and you think they're just going to trust one of your lot?"

"I don't think, I *know*."

Janine gritted her teeth. "I hate it when you're cryptic."

"Tough tits. The mother's in Moon's clinic, in case you were wondering about someone other than yourself."

"You cheeky fuck. Can I speak to her?"

"No. She'll be going to rehab after she's been checked over. She needs help."

Janine thought of the postmortem report. "Drugs and drink."

"Yep, plus the matter of a pimp we need to get her away from. She'll be relocated."

"Okay, I'll let her slide. Just give me Luke's killers. Do what you like to the pimp, I don't want him. I assume it's a him."

"You assumed right. Chat later, tater."

Despite the situation, she laughed at his sign-off and put the phone in her pocket. Digested what she'd learned. Once again, she was going to have to act as if she didn't know the killers had been apprehended by The Brothers. And once again, she'd have to act shocked when she was called out to view their bodies.

Fuck's sake.

Chapter Eleven

Stephanie wasn't at work on Monday morning. Had she stayed off because her face was so bruised? Pippa had spent the rest of the weekend worrying about a knock on the door from the police, but none had come. She'd also worried that only Fiona and Theresa had received visits, because they'd been the ones to do most of the assault. Lillibet had delivered a kick, but Stephanie might not have registered that as she'd been in pain from the other two attacking her. She wouldn't have known Pippa had kicked her in the ribs, just that someone had, because she had been too out of it to cotton on.

Pippa glanced over at Fiona who sipped coffee at her desk. Theresa read something on her monitor, and Lillibet flicked through files. They'd agreed to act normal at work, to not mention it in case Mr Ford overheard them at any point, but Pippa couldn't stand it. She didn't have their phone numbers so couldn't have rung or messaged them on Sunday, and emails today were out of the question. Mr Ford could read all of them as they were always automatically blind copied to another account only he had access to.

Pippa thought about the email Fiona had sent, asking her to go to the pub last Monday for a chat. Thankfully, it hadn't contained anything ominous, but would the police, should they become involved, want to know what they'd needed to chat about?

The hours crawled by. Lunchtime arrived, and instead of going to her usual spot by the fountain, Pippa tagged along to the Old Woodshed with the others. Drinks bought and food ordered, they sat in a secluded spot away from customers.

"It's been hell not talking about this," Fiona said.

Pippa nodded. "I've been shitting myself all day so far. How can we find out what's going on without it seeming suss?"

Theresa sipped her orange juice. "I'm at the end of a project. I can go and ask Mr Ford if he wants me to send it to him direct, seeing as Stephanie isn't here to proofread it. He might say why she's off."

"There's been nothing on the news," Lillibet said.

"She's probably kept her gob shut like I told her to." Fiona clamped her lips as a server had come with their food.

While they ate, Pippa fretted. She'd wanted to be friends with these three for a long time, and now she was, she regretted getting involved. She'd been so desperate to belong that she hadn't backed out of the plan to hurt Stephanie, and now look.

Lunch break over, they wandered back to the office. Stepping off the lift first, Pippa halted, one of the others bumping into her back.

"Blimey," Lillibet said. "You could have warned me you were stopping."

Pippa took a couple of steps forward, then realised she likely came off as weird, gawping, so she walked to her desk as if having a police officer in uniform, plus a man in a suit speaking to Mr Ford, wasn't unusual at work. She sat, her chest seeming hollow, her heartbeat rattling around in there. Fiona, Theresa, and Lillibet went to their desks, although they cast low glances at each other every so often.

"Let me just ask them," Mr Ford said, louder than the previously mumbled conversation between them. He walked over and stood by Fiona's desk. "Detective Inspector Rod Clarke is here with PC Harlech to ask a few questions about Stephanie. She didn't call in sick this morning, which was odd, and now I understand why."

Pippa's pulse thudded in her head.

Mr Ford wafted a hand, giving the police the floor. "I'll let you explain things."

Rod moved to stand beside the boss. "If we could have a chat to you one by one, that would be great."

"What about?" Theresa asked.

"Stephanie." Rod scratched his head. "Mr Ford has said we can use the meeting room, so who'd like to go first?"

Pippa raised a hand. "Can it be me? I've got a lot of work and need to crack on with it." She flicked through the plan in her head, reminding herself of what they'd agreed to say.

"Yep." Rod wandered off into the meeting room with Harlech.

Mr Ford folded his arms. "Off you go, then, Pippa."

She got up and, on noodle legs, went into the office while Ford went into his. She closed the door and sat at the long table. Rod, sitting on the other side of it, steepled his hands, his elbows on the shiny wood. Harlech leaned against the left-hand wall beside a grey filing cabinet.

"Can I start with your full name, please?" Rod asked.

Pippa stared at his yellow-tinged, tombstone teeth and unkempt appearance. It didn't seem like he showered very often, and he stank of staleness, reminding her of the old man by the fountain.

"Pippa King."

"Have you worked here long?"

"Six months."

Harlech wrote in his notebook, and Pippa hid a squirm.

"How well do you know Stephanie Rogers?" Rod asked.

"Not very. She's got the desk next to mine, but we don't talk much. She keeps herself to herself. Has she done something wrong?"

"Not as far as we're aware." Rod displayed his teeth, stretching his lips back. "When did you last see her?"

On the floor, barely breathing. *"Friday, here."*

"Right. And how did she seem?"

"Normal. Quiet."

"I see. Where were you on Saturday night?"

Pippa blinked, knowing the answer she must give, but her mouth wouldn't form those words. Instead, she said, "What do you need to know that for?"

"Just answer the question, Miss King."

"I met up with the others."

"And they are?"

"Fiona, Theresa, and Lillibet."

"Where did you go?"

"First off was The Bar—I got a taxi from my place and met them there about eight. Then we went to The Wheatsheaf, then Cuban Cocktails. We got a taxi after that to The Lion."

"Which Lion?"

"The one on Bold Street."

Rod rested one hand on the table and pinched his chin with the finger and thumb of the other. "Close to where Stephanie's house is. Interesting."

Pippa's internal thermostat went haywire, and she prayed her face wouldn't turn red. "I don't know where she lives so can't say."

"That's convenient."

"What? I'm telling the truth!"

Rod eyed her. "How long were you in The Lion?"

"A couple of hours."

"What time did you leave?"

"We got a cab at last orders and went to The Roxy."

"Ah, I know it well. The club by The Angel?"

"Yes."

"When did you leave there?"

"God, it must have been about two. We had kebabs from the van round the corner."

Rod nodded. "What next?"

"We got taxis home. We shared a black cab. I got dropped off first."

"And where do you live?"

"Fifteen Marquis Road."

"In one of the flats?"

"Yes."

"They call it Shoebox City down there on account of the flats not being big enough to swing a cat, did you know that?"

What the fuck has that got to do with anything? *"No."*

"So, to clarify, you didn't see Stephanie at any point during your night out?"

Had someone seen them? Identified them? Was this a test?

Stick to the plan. *"No, like I said, I last saw her on Friday."*

143

Rod swung his chair from side to side. "Do you know if any of the other girls here have a grudge against her?"

"A grudge? Why would they? Stephanie's quiet, gets on with her job."

"She's dead."

Pippa's world spun out of control. The room tilted, and she gripped the chair arms to steady herself. "What?"

"She was attacked in her home on Saturday night. You wouldn't happen to know anything about that, would you?"

"No! Oh my God, this is horrible." We killed her. We bloody killed her!

"Beaten to death," Rod went on, like this kind of chat was an everyday thing for him. *"Kicked mostly. The pathologist said a particularly savage kick to the head was what killed her. Fluid on the brain. Swelling."*

Pippa swallowed, bile burning her tongue. "Who…who would do that?"

"This is what we aim to find out. Did she ever discuss the church with you?"

"No."

"So you're saying you know sod all about her and can't help me."

Pippa shrugged. "Sorry, but I can't tell you anything if I don't know. She didn't speak to me about her life, we just chatted about work. Do you think someone from the church beat her up or something?"

"It's an angle. When you go back out there, do not *discuss this conversation with your colleagues until we've gone. I like the element of surprise when delivering the news. You giving the others a heads-up means they have a chance to concoct a story."*

"They wouldn't have done this!"

"Hmm. Okay, that's all. Send the next one in, will you?"

His abrupt dismissal of her couldn't have come soon enough. Pippa rose and walked out, hoping she didn't trip—her legs had gone numb. She chose Theresa and told her to go into the meeting room. Once the door shut, Pippa sagged into her chair and held her face in her hands.

"What did he say?" Fiona whisper-hissed.

Pippa lowered her hands and linked her fingers to stop them from shaking. "He told me not to say anything." She hated this. She wanted to blurt it out, not carry this burden until they'd all been told.

"You look like you want to throw up. Is it bad?"

Pippa nodded and swallowed again. "I can't…"

She rushed to the toilet and locked herself in a cubicle. Thankfully, neither Fiona nor Lillibet followed, likely thinking it would look bad if Rod found them all clustered in the loo. She put the seat lid down and sat on it, taking in huge breaths. What if one of the others fucked up? What if something slipped out and got them in trouble? Would Pippa be in the shit, even though she hadn't done anything except kick Stephanie once? Rod had said brain swelling—who had kicked her in the head the most? Which kick had killed her, or was it a combination of all of them? How did the police establish which woman was responsible? Did it even work like that, or would they be tried as a gang, all charged with murder?

She stood, left the cubicle, and washed her face. Stared at herself in the mirror above the two sinks. Did she look guilty? Or just shocked?

She returned to the office. Theresa had come back out, and she sat at her desk, crying. Lillibet had gone in, and Fiona picked at her nails. Pippa went over to Theresa and crouched beside her.

"What the fuck are we going to do?" Theresa whispered, glancing at Fiona to check if she strained to listen.

"I don't know."

"He asked where we'd been and everything."

"Same."

"He kept saying about her church. St Matthew's. As if we'd know whether she had a beef with someone there." Theresa's voice went even lower. *"What if they check her home laptop or whatever and find those emails she sent? The police will come back to ask us about them."*

"Then you say it was a strange incident that happened to all of you but you had no idea who sent them."

Theresa rubbed at her face. "I didn't expect her to die."

"None of us did. We stick together, okay?"

Theresa nodded just as Lillibet came out of the office. Skin pale, hands shaking by her sides, she navigated to her desk and sat, staring at her computer screen.

"Fucking hell…"

"What?" Fiona said. "This is doing my head in, not knowing."

"Go in there," Lillibet snapped. "Then you'll *know an' all. This was all your stupid idea anyway…"*

Pippa didn't think that was fair. Lillibet had been all for it during the planning stage.

At her desk, Pippa waited for Fiona to come back. Fifteen long minutes later, she emerged, visibly shaken. She sat, avoiding all eye contact until Rod and Harlech had left, Mr Ford showing them out.

"Oh my fucking God," Fiona said. "We stick by our stories, understand? We keep the secret, no matter how hard it is."

Everyone else nodded.

Chapter Twelve

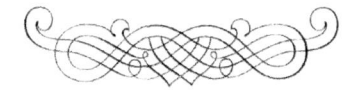

The office door stood ajar. Nessa approached it, wary. For all she knew, Chesney had opened it for her so he could return to sit by his mother rather than get up to let her in, but what if, in the meantime, thugs had arrived and raided the place for drugs—and were still in there?

Don't be stupid.

Nervous, she popped her head around the edge, ready to make a run for it if need be. She shouldn't have worried. Chesney sat on the floor, his knees drawn up, hugging them. Beside him, an out-for-the-count Marlborough, her cheeks a mess of burnt flesh. Chesney stared at nothing and appeared so childlike she almost felt sorry for him. *Almost*. Then she remembered the baby and Pippa, and all sympathy flew out of the window. He wasn't the brightest bulb in the chandelier it seemed, as he rocked backwards and forwards slightly instead of trying to wake Marlborough up. He didn't seem to have heard Nessa come in, so she walked inside and shut the door loudly.

It snapped him out of his trance, and he stared at her as if his brain was empty. Redness rimmed his eyes, and watery snot dribbled from one nostril. He cuffed it absently, blinking. "Oh. It's you."

"Expecting someone else, were you?"

"No."

Nessa couldn't bear to look at him at the minute so stared at the top of his head. Just the sight of him pissed her off—and got her so angry at Dickie for having another kid who clearly wasn't cut out for catastrophes. He'd panicked with Pippa, which had resulted in a baby's death, and was currently so shocked at his mother being attacked that he didn't do anything but sit there feeling sorry for himself.

No wonder Marlborough said they needed me in their firm. I wouldn't trust this gimp to open a packet of crisps without spilling them.

Her work phone bleeped, so she retreated outside and read the message.

GG: News just came in. Ask him if he murdered Father Dublin and some woman called Hazel at St Matthew's this morning.

What? Nessa's stomach dropped. Were the twins sure it was him or just fishing? Chesney didn't have any blood on him. Had he put overalls on? Did he have a gun? Now? Would he use it on her if she did something he didn't like? So many questions rushed through her mind that she had to shut them off.

Nessa: Fuck me! I'll kill the little bastard.

GG: I'd rather you didn't. That's our job. <laughing emoji>

Nessa: I'm going in now.

Another response, this time with the safe house address, where to find the keys, and the instruction to hang around for a while before she went there so someone had a chance to drop the keys off and get out of sight.

She slid her phone away and entered the office, closing the door. "Where were you this morning?"

He shook his head. "What?"

"I don't think I sounded foreign, did I? I mean, I reckon I said that clearly enough."

Chesney flushed and stood, seeming to fully knock himself out of whatever daze he'd been in. "Fuck what I was doing, we need to get Mum some help."

So now he's bothered.

Nessa diverted her attention to Marlborough. "Where do you propose we take her? If it's a hospital, they're going to ask questions—and what are you going to say? If a nurse phones the police, you'll be fucked, what with keeping that woman here. And why is your mum still unconscious? Are you sure she's not dead?"

Chesney jumped from the shock of her words. "Oh God…" He dropped to his knees to check her pulse. "She's alive. She's all right." He pushed to his feet again and walked over to flump onto a desk chair. "Do you know someone who could help?"

Nessa feigned thinking. She nodded. "Yes, one of my friends used to be a nurse. I'll ring her in a minute. But first, tell me what you were up to before you came here."

He eyed her funny. "Why do you need to know?"

"Because I drove past St Matthew's and saw plod outside."

Chesney swallowed. "Shit. I knew I should have locked that door."

"So you *were* there."

"I had to get rid of the priest, didn't I. He was a prick and told the pigs a woman brought the baby to him. It wouldn't have been long before the police twigged it wasn't a woman but a man. Anyway, he needed to learn his lesson for opening his big gob and disobeying me."

She pretended she didn't know anything. "There's something you're not saying, I can tell."

He pulled a Tesco carrier bag over and poked around inside it. Took out a sandwich and ripped the front of the packaging off. Was he for real? His mum was out of it on the floor, and he was going to *eat* like the situation was normal? He took after Dickie for something, then, putting himself first.

"Didn't have breakfast," he said, as if that explanation justified his actions. He bit into one half of the sandwich and chewed loudly.

"So what else have you left out?" she asked. "If you want my help, I need to know everything. I can't go into this without all the facts."

He swallowed and sighed. "There was this old biddy there, all right? At the church. I'd just put a bullet in Dublin's head, and she turns up, hands on her hips like I'm some naughty boy. I'm not, I'm a man."

You keep convincing yourself of that, mate.

Nessa tapped her foot. "And?"

"I shot her."

"Oh, great. Did you not think you're in enough shit as it is without killing two more people? And the mother of that baby is out there doing God knows what, speaking to God knows who. What's her name?"

"Pippa."

"Right, well, Pippa's bound to go and tell someone about what you've done to her and the baby. Whether it's someone she's friends with, The Brothers, or the police, I don't know, but we can't stay here, and you can't go home. We need to go somewhere else until it's all blown over."

"We'll go to your flat above the Noodle."

"We fucking won't." She made out like she racked her brains. "Okay, listen, I've got a house no one knows about, I lived there before I got the job at the Noodle. Dickie bought it for me a couple of years ago. He used to store stuff there until he got his lock-up. I was thinking of renting it out but never got round to it. Glad I didn't now, because it'll be handy for us to hole up in. I'll get my friend to come and see your mum there."

Chesney had finished the sandwich and poked around in the bag again, producing a small bottle of orange and a granola bar that had likely come with a meal deal. "All right." He drank the juice in several gulps, stuffed the bar in his pocket, then stood. "What about Pippa?"

"We'll make proper plans once we're out of here. Are there any drugs about?"

"Eh?"

She resisted screaming at him to get his head in the game. "In here, any drugs?"

"Oh. In the safe. They'll be all right."

"They won't if Pippa tells the police about this place and it gets raided. *Think*, Chesney!"

"It's in Dad's name, so they'll think they're his?" He sounded as if he clutched at straws.

"But if he left the office to your mum, the coppers are going to come knocking at her house. They'll see the state of her."

Chesney's mind seemed to tick over. A calculating look passed over his pale face. "Did he? Leave it to her, I mean?"

"I don't know, the will hasn't been read yet." Frustration built, and Nessa had the urge to walk out and leave him to deal with this on his own. "It doesn't matter, just get the bloody drugs and help me carry your mum to my car."

"What about mine and Mum's? The police will see them."

Nessa sighed. "Give me the keys. I'll stop by the Noodle on our way to the house and get two of my staff to come and collect them."

"Can we trust them?"

"Of course we fucking can else I wouldn't have mentioned them. God!"

He remained sitting.

"Get a move on, then!" she shouted.

Chesney shot up and went to the safe, taking a podgy carrier bag out. He went to pass it to her, and she held her hands up.

"I'm not touching that. Go and put it in my car. Hurry up!"

He disappeared outside, and Nessa stared down at Marlborough. Christ, she didn't even know her first name, Mum had always referred to her as 'that Marlborough bitch'. Nessa bent to hook her hands beneath the woman's armpits and dragged her towards the door, glancing away from the wrecked face. Chesney returned and picked up his mum's ankles, and they hefted her outside and onto the back seat.

"Lock the office up while I make sure she's lying down," Nessa said. "We don't want anyone seeing her."

Chesney scuttled off. Nessa stretched Marlborough out, tucked her legs up, then got into the driver's side. She drummed her fingertips on the steering wheel, getting more annoyed with every second that passed. What the fuck was he *doing* in there? She tooted the horn, contemplating driving off and leaving him, but The Brothers wanted mother *and* son, so no matter how much he bugged her, she had to take him with her.

Chesney finally came out, locked the door, and slid into the passenger side. Nessa drove to the Noodle, glad he didn't want to talk, and put the car keys in her safe with no intention of asking anyone to collect the vehicles—the twins would want to do that. Back in her car, she stuck the satnav on and put in the safe house address.

"Don't you know where your own house is?" Chesney asked.

Shit. "It's been ages since I was there. Last year sometime."

He seemed to accept that explanation. "Wonder why Dad didn't buy *me* a house."

Nessa set off, following the satnav directions. "No idea. Maybe he has but didn't get around to giving it to you. We'll soon know when the will's read."

"When's that?"

"No clue. Now shut up and let me think."

"What about?"

"How to keep you and your mum out of the shit if the police go to that office and find evidence Pippa was there." She laughed to get him thinking she was as deranged as Dickie. "I know, I'll find her and see if she's told anyone, then I'll kill her."

He stroked the seat belt absently. "What if she *has* spilled the beans?"

"Then I'll kill whoever she told an' all."

Chesney let out a long breath. "Shit, sounds like you're *worse* than Dickie."

"The apple doesn't fall far from the tree," she lied. She was *nothing* like Dickie. She hoped.

"Eh? What are you *on* about? What do the apples mean?"

"Doesn't matter. Now be quiet."

The rest of the journey made in silence, Nessa turned up a track that led to a building surrounded by trees. A cottage, sandstone, with old-fashioned sash windows and what appeared to be a recent new roof. She parked and got out, walking up to an ornamental dark-grey stone in a rockery beside a potted miniature fir tree beside the front door. She dropped her phone on purpose, crouching to pick it up, and took the key from beneath the stone, otherwise Chesney would likely ask why she didn't have a set of keys for her own property. She opened the door and pushed it wide, then returned to the car.

Back door open, she poked her head in. "Don't just sit there! Help me get your mum indoors."

They carried the still-sleeping woman into the cottage, Nessa opting for the first room on the right. A kitchen.

She cursed not knowing the layout and chuffed out an embarrassed laugh. "Bloody hell, the living room's at the back. Got it confused with my mum's house for a minute there."

He was going to cotton on that she'd never been here before if she didn't get her head on straight. They placed Marlborough on one of the sofas. Nessa took a throw blanket off the back and covered her with it.

"Right, I'll go and lock my car then phone my mate. There's coffee and whatever in the cupboards." She prayed there was.

Outside, she closed the car doors and clicked the key fob. Used her work phone and acted as if she touched the screen to contact her so-called nurse pal. In case Chesney watched and listened from the kitchen, she put the mobile to her ear and said, "Hi, it's Nessa. Can you do me a favour and come to my house? Yeah, the one my dad bought for me. I've got a burnt woman here, her face is a mess, and she's been unconscious for a while. An hour? That's great. Cheers, love."

Inside, she found Chesney putting a kettle on to boil, two cups out on the worktop. He flicked the switch and turned to look at her.

"She'll be here in an hour," Nessa said.

He nodded. "Thank God for that."

Chapter Thirteen

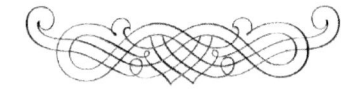

Stephanie's death had hit the news the day after the police had been to the office. Journalists had arrived outside the building, and when Pippa had left work that Tuesday, they'd shouted questions at her, one of the press pack shoving a microphone under her nose. She'd scurried down the street, head bent, and jumped onto a bus, not caring that it was going in the

wrong direction. She'd had to get away, to distance herself.

A month had passed since then. She'd spent most evenings drinking bottles of wine to blot everything out, and on Saturday nights, she'd met with the others, going bar-hopping and having sex with whoever approached her. Last weekend, she'd had five hundred pounds left on the credit card and had blown the lot. One last bender before she got a grip on herself.

She had nothing but her wages coming in and no means to pay the first credit card bill. She should have kept some back from that final five hundred. Too late to do anything about it now. That cash had been banked by the various pubs she'd squandered it in, buying drinks for her friends and whoever else had tagged along with them. She'd paid for them all to get into The Roxy, too, determined to have an ace night, one she'd never forget.

Another Monday had rolled round, and she walked into work, still with a thick head—she'd spent her Sunday on the sofa beneath a blanket, paracetamol and her flask of tea to hand. Hangovers had become worse the more she drank, and every day, after the evening wine sessions, she felt herself slipping farther into 'bad employee' territory. Mr Ford hadn't called her into his office yet, but it wouldn't be long before he did.

An older woman called Rachel had taken Stephanie's job. She was the life and soul, eager to get along with everyone, and she brightened up the place. The problem was, Stephanie's death had affected everyone, all of them becoming subdued, so Rachel appeared confused half the time as to why her jokes didn't get laughed at.

"Morning!" Rachel trilled, carrying a tray of hot drinks through from the break room. She deposited a mug on each desk, then popped the tray beside hers and sat. "Have a good weekend?"

"Another Saturday getting drunk," Fiona said.

Rachel laughed. "You're all terrible, I tell you. I sat watching telly with my dog."

Pippa wished she'd done the same, except she didn't have a dog, only Bear for company. She wouldn't have spent the last of the money if she'd stayed in. She wouldn't have the worry of how she'd find the cash to pay that first bill.

She sat and thought about it, tuning Rachel's chatter out. What if she paid the bill out of her utilities pot, waited for it to clear, then withdrew it off the card again? Pleased she'd found a solution—relieved would be a better word—she forced herself to get into her work.

Fiona interrupted Pippa's concentration with, "Are you up for Saturday night, Pip?"

"I'm skint," she said. She'd already decided to cut ties with them, so revealing her poor status didn't bother her now.

"I should think so, considering what you spent last time." Fiona leaned back. "What about buying wine and drinking it before we go out?"

"I'm literally skint, as in, proper in the shit. I've got nothing except bill money left. You lot go and have a nice time for me."

"Can't you get a sub from your parents?"

I don't have Mummy and Daddy to fall back on like you do. *"No, they don't lend me money, never have, and if I went to them and asked for cash to get pissed, they'd tell me to find another job that pays better."*

"Oh. All right, then."

Relief once again pounding through her, Pippa opened a new document and got on with adding the current client's information. She'd have to play this carefully, easing herself away from the group.

"How come you're tight for cash, though?" Fiona pressed.

Pippa was going to have to lie. "My rent went up. They want a hundred more every month."

"What, for a shoebox?"

That reminded her of Rod, and she shook away images of the copper. "London prices." She smiled. "It's fine, honestly. I've been a bit of a party animal, so I could do with a rest from the booze."

But she wouldn't give up the booze. She was already working out how many bottles of wine she could buy if she scrimped on food.

Fiona had let it go eventually. Pippa hadn't been out with them for five Saturdays in a row, but Rachel had taken her place. Pippa worried that, in a drunken moment, one of the others would blurt out what they'd done to Stephanie. Maybe moving away was the best bet, changing jobs, too. Creating so much distance between them that they forgot about her. But that meant finding a new bond for a flat, plus a month's rent in advance, and she couldn't do it.

The second credit card bill had arrived.

And she couldn't pay it, she'd spent too much on wine.

Shit.

In the four months since Stephanie's death, Pippa had to admit she was likely an alcoholic now. Drink consumed her thoughts—how to afford it, how to get her hands on it, how to drink it without anyone knowing what she was doing. Tea no longer filled her lunch flask, wine mixed with vodka did. Her nightmares about the murder had filtered into her waking moments, and she saw Stephanie everywhere she went. Not her, exactly, but parts of her on other people. The eyes on one woman, the nose on another, and that horrible smirk of hers on a third. Her hair, her walk, her everything. It was driving Pippa mad.

She'd missed the last three payments on the credit card. She'd ignored all the red demands, and this morning, one from a bailiff had arrived. She was behind a month on her rent, promising her landlord she'd play catch-up. Her electricity had been cut off.

It was Friday and, lying on her sofa in the dark, her wine and vodka concoction almost gone, she contemplated going to the off-licence again. She had three hours before bed, and she couldn't hack that without alcohol—couldn't drift off to sleep without it anyway. She downed the rest of her glass and took the last twenty quid that was supposed to be for food next week, nipping out onto the landing, wary of seeing any neighbours. The bloke next door was all right, but the others not so much. They gave her filthy looks, like they knew she was an alchie, and the shame always poured into her then.

She wandered up the road, and it took her a moment to realise she hadn't put her shoes on. Bobbles of tarmac dug into her feet, but she stumbled on, too desperate for drink to care. She pushed into the shop, bumping into some woman with her little girl.

"Sorry," she mumbled.

"Jesus Christ, love, at least eat mints to disguise it."

Embarrassed, Pippa went straight to the alcohol section, picked up a large bottle of white, then went to the counter to ask for vodka from the cabinet behind. The assistant's stare burned into her, and she felt his disdain, how gross he thought she was. She paid, rushing out of the shop and onto the street and, too desperate to wait until she got home, she put the wine on a nearby wall and unscrewed the vodka cap. She took a long, burning swig, and immediately calmed.

Back at home, she mixed the two drinks together in her glass and settled in the darkness, no telly to watch, no fire to put on—what a fucking sorry state of affairs. Feeling sorry for herself and needing to get warm, she guzzled her whole glass, stuck her shoes on, and snatched the fiver change from the twenty, stuffing it in her jeans pocket.

Outside once again, she ran to the nearest pub, her eyes hot from tears, a lump in her throat. She sloped inside and approached the bar, asking for a lager. The barmaid eyed her funny, as if she thought she was too drunk to serve, then shrugged and pulled the pint. Pippa handed the cash over and drank deeply, then stopped herself. She'd have to eke the rest out in order to stay here in the warm.

Exhausted emotionally, she slumped onto a bar stool.

A man sidled up to her and gave her a nudge. "You look rough as fuck."

She didn't have any dignity or self-care left in her to retaliate. Who cared what he thought of her? Yes, she was aware she looked a mess without makeup to hide the bags under her eyes and cover her bad skin. Yes, she knew she didn't smell too nice. And yes, she was rough as fuck. So. Fucking. What?

"Piss off," she muttered, "and leave me alone."

"A problem shared an' all that." He sat on a stool beside her. "Come on, what's happened to get you in this state?"

She let it tumble out—the booze addiction, the lack of money, the bailiff letter, no electricity, and all the other shit she coped with, but not about the murder, never that. No matter how drunk she got, she'd never confess to being a part of it.

"What would you say if I said I could help you out of that hole?" he asked.

She chuffed out her derision. "Yeah, right."

"Straight up. I could lend you money to get everyone off your case, then you can work for me, pay me back that way."

"Doing what?"

"You don't need to worry yourself about that just yet. What about coming to my place? I've got a much better alternative to make all your troubles float away."

"Sex isn't going to work."

"I didn't mean sex."

Later, on his sofa, after he'd worn her down by keep encouraging her to take it, Pippa experienced the first effects of cocaine, her new best friend.

Chapter Fourteen

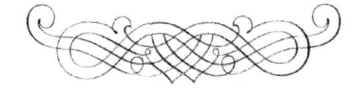

Debbie happened to be in The Angel and not at Moon's house when George and Greg turned up, approaching the bar with poker faces. She finished serving her customer and waved away his payment so she could get to the twins faster.

"What's the matter?" she asked quietly, gripping the Guinness pump handle, readying herself for a catastrophe to land in her lap.

"We'll chat in your old room in the parlour," George said.

So it was something they didn't want anyone overhearing, then. Something serious. She followed them down there, nodded to Amaryllis who manned the reception desk, and went into the spare room. To the outsider, massages occurred here, but to those in the know, her girls entertained punters in a different way entirely. She used to be one of those girls.

She closed the door. Leaned on it. Had already twigged by their expressions they wanted her for something or other.

"What do you need me to do?" She almost sighed but held it back. She shouldn't be naffed off if the twins asked her to help with jobs from time to time, they'd been bloody good to her, but since she'd started seeing Moon, she'd taken her foot off the gas and quite enjoyed her new life as a lady of leisure and luxury.

"Is it that obvious?" George sat and leaned back.

Greg plonked himself down opposite. "We've got a bit of a problem and need you to act as a decoy."

"A decoy?" she asked.

"Yeah, a nurse." George smirked.

Debbie laughed. "Those days are gone, love. I don't do sex work anymore, you know that, and the only person I dress up for in the bedroom is Moon."

"Not in *that* way." George sniffed. "And that was too much information. You don't even need a uniform on."

"Why a nurse?"

"Because some woman's got a baked face from having boiled water poured on it. You have to go in and make out you're going to fix it. Or give her some ointment or something."

"Was it you two who did that?"

"Nope. Someone else had the honour."

Debbie was known around here, so asked, "What if this person knows who I am?"

"You've kept your past under your hat, so say you used to be a nurse in a former life. Whatever, we just want you to go in the front of the house while we go in the side. If a certain pair of arseholes see us getting out of the van, things will go tits up, so you're the distraction."

"Your *van*?"

"Yeah."

"You expect me to drive that beaten-up piece of shit?"

George bristled. "We've had that van years. She's special to us."

"She?" Debbie chortled. "I've heard it all now. Got a name, has she?"

George grinned. "Piss off. And so what if she has? So, cancel all plans, because you're coming with us."

"Am I in danger when we get there? Moon won't like it if I am."

"Nope, because as far as the bloke's concerned, you're Nessa Feathers' friend."

"Nessa, from the Noodle?"

"Yeah."

"What the hell's *she* got herself into?"

George told what Debbie gathered was a short version of the story.

"Shit, that baby…" Her legs went wobbly, and she moved across to sit beside Greg. "God, what a bloody shame. So the mother's going to rehab, you said. What about her pimp?"

"We're getting him and his right-hand man later. Do you know him? Goes by the name of Crook."

"Oh, *that* prick. He used to come in the pub a couple of years ago, but he wasn't called Crook then, just used his real name."

"Which is?"

"Bartholemew Astor."

"Jesus," Greg muttered, "no wonder he picked Crook instead. He sounds posh."

"Nah, he's common as muck," Debbie said.

"What does he look like?" George asked.

"Short dark hair, bit of a Tom Hardy sort. I'm surprised you two haven't heard of him, although it's a big estate, so I'll let you off."

George chuckled. "Hark at her, Greg. She'll let us off. Good job we love her, else I'd get offended by her saying that."

Debbie sighed out to release the tension in her chest. She'd seen the news about the abandoned baby so had known the twins would be on it at some point. "This is all a bit of a pickle, isn't it. When will people learn not to do shit behind your backs? You always catch up with them in the end. Drugs with this Chesney and his mum, pimping with Crook. And what are you going to do about the sex workers on Kitchen Street? That was where you said they worked, didn't you? With Crook gone, they'll have no one to look after them—if he even did."

George shrugged. "Feel free to take them on yourself."

"I will. It's only a couple of streets away. We'll get a watcher down there to keep them safe and whatnot." And there Debbie had been, liking her life of leisure, yet a spark lit inside her at the idea of getting back into things. New girls, a new corner…she loved to nurture, so this was ideal, especially as Moon was going away on business abroad soon. She didn't want to know what he was up to, and immersing herself in welcoming those women into the fold would take her mind away from thinking about him.

"Come on, then." Greg stood. "We'll go over the plan on the way."

They left the room. Debbie grabbed one of the first-aid kits behind the reception desk. Amaryllis didn't ask questions, she never did, but going by her face, she knew something big was up.

It didn't take long for Debbie to drive the van to the safe house, although she cursed the sticking gears. "You need to put this bloody thing in for a service before your clutch goes," she grumbled to George and Greg lying in the back.

"A mechanic now, are you?" George asked.

"No, but it's obvious it's on its way out." She turned onto the track, eyeing a car parked out the front of the cottage. "Looks like I've got a welcome committee. Nessa and some little scrote have come out on the doorstep. I'm sure I've seen him in The Angel."

"Toasty Face isn't with them, then?" George asked.

"No. Shut up now, else they'll see my mouth moving and twig you're in here." She parked up and got out, carrying the kit and feeling a right dickhead as it likely didn't even contain the things a nurse would use on a burn victim.

Nessa stepped forward and hugged her as if they were long-lost mates. She whispered in her ear, "He's got room temperature IQ, so nothing to worry about."

Debbie held in a snort of laughter and drew back. "How are you? Long time no see."

"Oi, aren't you that bird from The Angel?" Chesney walked towards them, a frown creasing his features.

So much for a low IQ.

"What the fuck's going on?" he demanded.

Debbie glared at him, didn't like his attitude. "I am Debbie, yes. I was a nurse years ago. Got a problem with that?" She raised her eyebrows. "If I'm here, it means you don't want to take your mother to a hospital, so it's in your best interests not to speak to me like that—your tone stinks. And pull your manners out of your arse where you shoved them, otherwise I'm fucking off and leaving you to it."

"Sorry," he said.

"So you should be. Now let me see to your mum."

Chesney sloped indoors, and Debbie glanced at Nessa who rolled her eyes. Seemed she'd been having a time of it with her half-brother. Debbie had been surprised about the fact they were related when George had mentioned that snippet.

"Fucking little dick," Nessa whispered. "He's driving me insane. Why Dickie thought to bring him into his business is beyond me."

"Maybe he was going to teach him how to behave but didn't get the chance."

Nessa shook her head. "Even if taught, he wouldn't amount to much. He's been pampered all his life, I reckon."

Debbie followed her inside. Miss Marlborough, or Josephine as Debbie knew her when she'd been a customer in The Angel, had woken up and sat on the sofa, a blanket over her legs. The state of her face churned Debbie's stomach, but she kept the shock from her expression and approached. Placing the first-aid kid on the seat beside the woman, Debbie opened it, relieved to find a tube of burn salve as well as Germolene antiseptic cream and something for stings and bites, plus gauzes and whatnot.

"Go and wash your face as best you can," Debbie said to give The Brothers time to get into the cottage via the side door to the kitchen. They'd also instructed her to separate mother and son so it would be easier to round them up. "It needs cleansing first."

Josephine eyed her. "Debbie?" She stared at Nessa. "What the hell is *she* doing here? She's one of the twins' lot, for fuck's sake. Are you out of your mind?"

Debbie saved Nessa the burden of answering. "Like I told your son, I used to be a nurse, and watch your tone, got it?"

"I apologise, but you can understand my reservations." Josephine got up and shuffled from the room.

"Pat it dry, don't scrub," Debbie called after her.

Chesney flung himself on the other sofa. "You won't tell anyone about this, will you?" He bit a nail and spat it out.

Debbie snorted at his grossness. "The twins, you mean."

"Yeah. I thought you were well in with them."

"You thought wrong." Debbie went to the window and stared out as if admiring the surroundings. "I let people think what they want when it comes to those two."

"What's it like, working for them?" he asked.

"I don't. The Angel is mine, as is the corner. I work for no one."

"Oh. I didn't know that."

She turned to him. "I don't know why I'm here or how come your mum's face is fucked up, and I don't need to, but it tells me you're into some bad shit. I'll give you some advice." She continued, like George had told her to, so her cover appeared more genuine. "If you're up to stuff behind their backs, watch yourself. And if you're running some kind of dodgy business, then good luck to you, because when they find out, you won't be living for long."

"They know jack shit about what we do." Chesney laughed wryly. "They go around as if they're big hardmen, yet we've been operating under their noses for ages. Well, Mum and Dad were. I was only allowed to join in when I was eighteen."

"When was that?" Debbie asked. "Last week? Only, you're a bit green, it stands out a mile."

He folded his arms. "I'm doing my best."

In the corner of her eye, Debbie caught sight of George in the hallway. To get Nessa out of the way, she said, "Come and see this squirrel, Nessa. Daft bugger's rolling about in the grass."

Nessa walked to stand beside her. She must have copped on to George, too, as she stiffened and closed her eyes for a moment. Debbie casually spun round, giving the hallway a quick side glance. Greg crept up the stairs to waylay Josephine.

"What do you think about the news, Nessa?" Debbie asked. "That baby and everything. Bloody awful, isn't it?"

Nessa faced the same way as Debbie. "Hmm."

"What about you?" Debbie asked Chesney.

He blushed. "Err, yeah, terrible."

Debbie cocked her head. "So you feel bad for killing him, then?"

Chesney bolted upright and stared at Nessa. "Did you fucking *tell* her?"

"No!" Nessa said. "Christ, talk about jumpy."

"Wouldn't you be?" Chesney stood and paced in front of the sofa. "How did you know, Debbie? Who told you? Was I seen?"

"Word's got out, yes, *and* about the priest and that woman this morning."

Chesney stopped and stared her way, clearly crapping himself. "Did someone see me? I had a hood and sunglasses on. No way could anyone have recognised me."

"It was your car," Debbie said, teasing the confession out of him to save George the job of doing it at the warehouse. "Bit of a div move using that."

"Jesus," Chesney wailed. He came off as a five-year-old. "Do the police know? What have you heard?"

"Yes, they know." Debbie smiled towards the door.

George walked in. "And so do The Brothers. Time's up, sunshine. We're going for a little drive."

Chapter Fifteen

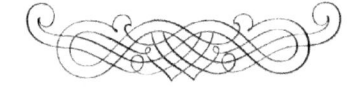

Pippa had been shown to a room on the ground floor. It was like a posh hotel, not rehab, and she sat on the wide bed, Will in an armchair by the bay window. She had a meeting with a consultant later, who'd go through the process with her. If he was to be believed, she'd be off drugs sooner than she'd thought if she was determined to get herself clean. She was. She'd never wanted to walk down the addict path, nor had she thought she'd sell her body for money, but she had. She'd never get over the shame of getting herself into debt, all for *things*. Stuff. Material crap that sat in her flat doing nothing but show how stupid she'd been, reminding her of it every day. And for what? When she hadn't been able to keep up with her friends and had got into debt, she'd turned to a new friend, drink.

"How come you're here?" Will asked.

"Because The Brothers want to help me out."

"No, why are you *here*. What happened in your life to get you to this point?"

She flushed, her cheeks getting hot. "Everything seems so *stupid* now. I was basically trying to fit in, to be something I'm not. I never belonged anywhere—or at least I didn't feel like I did—and I convinced myself that if I found friends to hang out with, everything would be okay. Except it wasn't. I got into so much debt I had a bailiff letter. I couldn't afford to pay my credit card, couldn't even get enough cash together to do one of those debt consolidation things."

"If you had no money, where did the drugs come into it?"

She snorted in disgust at herself. "I met Crook."

She told Will her story, minus the Stephanie shit, and relating it all now, she could see herself for the pathetic cow she'd been, desperate to be seen as someone worthy of being friends with, when all along, she should have just been herself, and if they didn't like her, tough.

"There was this old man, he tried to tell me, but I didn't listen. I should never have tried to squeeze myself into their mould." She sighed. "But I never did understand that people like them weren't right for me. The women at the office, I mean. There was this girl there, she suggested I go to the pub with her once, before I'd got in with all the others, and I remember looking at her and thinking: *You won't get me to where I need to be.* How up my own arse is *that*?"

"Has all this changed you?"

Pippa nodded. "Losing my baby..." Could she confess to how she'd really felt? Would Will judge her like she'd judged so many others? "I never wanted him, because of the rape, the circumstances. I didn't even know I was pregnant for ages. Yet when he came out of me and was dead... I wanted him so much, then. It was like I realised what a bitch I'd been, what was important, and I had a few days to think about my life, who I'd become, and decided that I'm not a nice person."

"Why weren't you nice? There must have been a reason for that."

"I could blame my childhood, but that was okay apart from being ignored. I was fed, clothed, didn't have it that bad. I must have been a cow deep inside for me to act like I did."

"The twins have got a therapist, you know. Vic. You could go and speak to him."

"I can't afford it."

"You don't need money for that. It's free because you live on Cardigan."

"I can't stick around here."

"Why not?"

"Even with Crook and Gopher gone, I still might be at risk. What if one of Crook's other workers comes after me?"

"Then move away."

Frustration bubbled. "What with, Monopoly money?"

Will shrugged. "George and Greg will sort it."

She pondered that. She already owed them so much, and Nessa, for being kind to her when she didn't deserve it. If they knew the real her, they might not be so nice. They'd see her as a right bitch and refuse to help. And Will was here, talking to her as if she wasn't the worst woman on the planet, even *after* she'd told him her story. There *were* some good people around, she'd just been too blind to see it, caught up in her own selfish needs.

She worried she wouldn't be able to turn over a new leaf, though. What if she was rotten to her core? No amount of pretending could hide that, could it? What if, when the hurt of her baby dying faded away, she slipped right back into who she'd been before?

"I think you should see Vic after you've come out of here," Will said. "You can kip at my flat if you don't feel safe in yours. I'll take you to his office and bring you back. He'll likely teach you how to be a better person."

Pippa stared into the middle distance and thought about that for a while. It wasn't like she had anything else to do, was it?

Chapter Sixteen

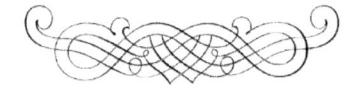

Chesney, naked in front of his *mother* of all people, sat strapped to a wooden chair by rope wound around his middle, his arms trapped by his sides. His hands throbbed from the pressure, the tightness of the bonds. Were they swollen? He didn't dare look down to check.

When he'd seen George in that house, his whole body had gone cold. Dad's number one rule in the business was that the twins couldn't know what they were up to, so knowing George did… Dad had wanted to get one over on them for forcing him into retirement. To prove they weren't as good as Ron Cardigan. To show they didn't deserve to run the estate if they didn't know what was happening right under their noses. George saying they were going for a little drive meant their warehouse. Dad had mentioned that—he'd been keeping tabs on them, watching them from time to time. Chesney had gathered the end was near, their lives on the line, and he'd tried to talk his way out of it.

George wasn't having any of it.

"Shut your lying fucking mouth," he'd said. "We know what you've been up to, and you're lucky we got to you first. If you went to prison as a baby killer… I don't need to spell it out, do I?"

One rash moment in his life meant Chesney had signed his own death warrant. He'd been so desperate to be like Dickie, to prove he had it in him to be a hardman, that his common sense had taken over on the night he'd shoved Pippa. How was he to know she was pregnant? She'd hardly had a bump. He'd thought the booze had bloated her.

He sighed, and his chest shuddered. Turning to Mum, he cursed himself for letting her down. Dad would never have made such a stupid mistake, and Chesney would bet Mum was thinking the same thing.

She sat on a foldable seat, also naked, although thankfully her boobs were covered with rope. He wouldn't be able to look at her if they were on show. She cried softly, tears tracking through the burns and popped blisters on her cheeks. They'd been positioned to face a long table, and as if this nudity wasn't indignity enough, George, Greg, Debbie, and Nessa ate McDonald's from Uber Eats. They acted as if Chesney and Mum weren't even there, chatting away about their lives, having a laugh, and generally behaving like two terrified people weren't starkers a few feet away.

Like this was *normal*.

He wanted to shout at them but couldn't. A wad of material filled his mouth, and he found it difficult to swallow, his saliva going AWOL on him. For the first time ever, he thought about mortality and how short life could be. He was eighteen, for fuck's sake, not eighty, and to suspect this was his last day on earth filled him with panic and a weird sense of loss—for who he could have been, the things he could have done, all of his dreams going unrealised.

Dad had told him he'd go far if he'd just listen and take note, that he'd become someone. He'd be a gangster with the best of them. *If* he thought before he acted. Chesney wished he'd done that with Pippa. Thought. Instead, he'd allowed anger to overtake him, fuelled by grief at his father's sudden death, the unfairness of losing him, and now he'd killed three people, one of them a tiny baby. He'd be paying for that soon, of that he had no doubt. And Mum had been dragged into the mess he'd created. She didn't deserve that.

Maybe the twins would listen if he pleaded her case. Would they let her go if he told them this was all down to him and nothing to do with her?

The journey to this warehouse had been a silent one—neither of the twins had spoken in the front of the van, Chesney and Mum tied up in the back. Nessa had driven Debbie here, who, it was clear now, hadn't been a nurse in a former life. Nessa had tricked them into thinking she was on their side, when all along she'd known the twins were coming to her house.

Was that even her house?

"So I told him to go and fuck himself with a sharp stick," George said. "No one offers me a kebab-flavoured Pot Noodle and gets away with it. That's just wrong on so many levels."

"If you *try* a kebab one, you might like it," Nessa said.

"Don't even go there." George scowled at her. "I've been going to that corner shop for *years*, and he knows I only get chicken and mushroom. And as for him trying to get me to buy Hovis bread and not a tiger loaf, well…"

Nessa glanced over at Chesney. She didn't appear to care that he, her *half-brother*, her *blood*, sat there hungry and scared out of his mind, while she dined on Big Macs. He tried to speak to her using his eyes, but she was dead behind hers. She didn't care about him, and to be honest, why would she? If their situations had been reversed, he was fucked if he'd give two shits. They didn't know each other, he hadn't been brought up with her, only hearing stories about her from Dad. To Nessa, Chesney was probably some little twat she couldn't wait to see the back of.

Her being nice to him when he'd gone to the wake at the Noodle must have been an act. Chesney had been horrible to her mother, and it hadn't bothered Nessa in the slightest. In fact, she'd kind of joined in. She'd already known about Pippa at that point, Mum had told her, so what had Nessa done, gone to The Brothers after, and they'd hatched this plan?

If there was one saving grace in all of this, he didn't have to worry about the police catching up with him for dumping the baby and killing Dublin and Hazel. No rapes in the prison showers or slices to his face with a homemade shiv. No being beaten up in his cell. No head forced into the toilet so he nearly drowned. Weird how that scared him more than imminent death. At least here, he knew it would come to an end. In prison, it would have gone on for years.

He tuned out the banter at the table and glanced at Mum. She stared back at him, more tears falling, and he wanted to hug her, to say sorry. For the most part, it had been him and her all the way, Dad only visiting once or twice a week as Chesney had been growing up. He'd sat with Dad on those evenings, but only until it was time for his parents to go out on the town about nine. Mum's sister had babysat him, staying over, Dad booking a posh hotel for them to sleep in after a meal and a show. He'd treated Mum like a princess, and Chesney had failed to do the same.

He tried to apologise to her, but the words sounded muffled.

If it wasn't for him, they wouldn't be sitting here, and that was something he'd regret right up until the second he died.

However soon that may be.

Josephine wanted to clout her son to kingdom come. She'd *told* Dickie that Chesney wasn't suited to this life, that he didn't have it in him to be a gangster, but the stubborn bastard had insisted he'd make a man out of him yet. Dickie had treated his son like a project, wanting him to be an extension of him. Someone to brag about. Now, she'd never have the chance to see him grow into his father's mould—Dickie wasn't here to teach him the ways, Nessa had betrayed them, and they were going to be killed, no question.

The other day, she'd had a sneaky feeling she shouldn't have trusted Nessa, no matter that Dickie had said his daughter would help them if push came to shove. From what Josephine had gathered by talking to others, Nessa and Dickie hadn't got on, yet to hear Dickie's side of it, you'd think they were inseparable. Maybe he hadn't wanted to admit he didn't have a bond with his child. That at forty, she'd forged her own path and veered away from him. When she'd taken on the management job at the Noodle, Dickie had been so proud, yet word went round that he'd regularly berated her, saying she'd fail.

Josephine had chosen to believe Dickie's version, but it was becoming clear that things weren't as he'd portrayed them. Nessa was as devious as him, she had a good head on her shoulders—she had to because she'd got the twins involved in this. What was she doing, getting back at Dickie now he was dead and he couldn't do anything about it?

At the crematorium, Josephine almost hadn't approached her, listening to her inner voice that warned her to deal with Pippa by herself, but then Dickie's rough, ghostly tones had barged into her head, warning her that the shit would hit the fan if Nessa didn't help them out. Josephine had walked forward and explained everything, and with Nessa agreeing to get them out of a bind, all the insecurities had seeped away.

Josephine was aware Nessa wasn't fond of her mother and would likely jump into the business with them just to piss her off, but Dickie had been wrong about contacting her if he wasn't around and things went wrong. He'd underestimated his firstborn. Nessa wasn't under his thumb like he'd thought.

A wave of grief walloped Josephine. God, she'd loved him.

For her sins. For all his faults. And hers, for believing everything he'd said. For going with a married man and being proud of it. Bragging that Dickie's wife couldn't keep him satisfied and she could. Often, she'd thought about why he hadn't left his marriage but had convinced herself he no longer slept with the woman he'd married.

She'd been stupid, hadn't she?

But despite everything, if he'd been here, Pippa would be six feet under and none of this would be happening. Chesney would have had the bollocking of his life from Dickie, who'd have slapped him about a bit to get some sense into his thick, immature head. Josephine could hear him now, ranting and raving.

"You pushed her and killed the fucking baby? What the hell's wrong *with you, son?"*

How different it would have been. Josephine hadn't cared about the baby's death, just that Chesney would be caught for bringing on the labour. Josephine would have been classed as an accessory, and their lives would never be the same. So of course they'd had to tie Pipa up and keep her gagged at the office until they'd worked out what to do with her. Maybe, if she'd approached Nessa sooner, the little cow wouldn't have gone to The Brothers.

Wishful thinking. There was no point in entertaining the what-ifs now. She had to deal with what was happening in front of her. The people who were going to kill her acted as if this scenario was an everyday occurrence. And it likely was. Maybe she could talk herself out of this. Her sister would be devastated when Josephine didn't come home.

More tears pooled, and she readied herself for the salty sting as they coasted down her face. Her nose was killing her from where Crook had punched it. Christ, that had hurt so much, and she'd blacked out, her last thought being that they'd probably murder her. To wake in that house with Chesney and Nessa had been a surprise, and upstairs, when she'd been in the middle of washing her sore face, the shock had come.

She'd lifted her head from over the bathroom sink and spotted one of the twins' reflections in the mirror above it. He'd glared at her then stalked into the room, snatching the back of her hair and twisting it around his fist.

"Fucking baby killer," he'd snarled.

"It…it wasn't me…"

His eyes had widened. "Go on, drop your son in it and tell me it was him. Show me who you *really* are, a woman ready to save her own arse."

What he'd said had brought her up short, because she *had* been about to tell him Chesney had done it. What sort of mother would that have made her? So she'd said *she'd* done it, her son hadn't even been there at the time, and the twin had revealed something that told her exactly what she'd been dying to know.

"Liar. Pippa came to us. We know everything."

And it had hit her then, that the two men who'd come to the office, the pimp and his scally, hadn't gone there because Pippa had informed them of where to go. She'd chosen The Brothers as her allies, not her pimp or the police, and in that moment, Josephine had realised this was the end. Crook would probably have just beaten her and Chesney up, the police would have thrown them in a holding cell and interrogated them, but the *twins*?

She wasn't getting out of here alive.

Chapter Seventeen

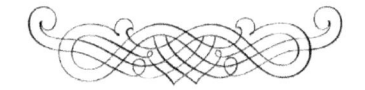

Leaving Ford and Sons hadn't been a hardship. Pippa had been relieved to walk out of there for the last time, away from her colleagues who'd distanced themselves from her when it had become apparent she'd taken the murder badly. She supposed they didn't want an unstable friend in their gang, although she did wonder why they weren't worried she'd open her

mouth and confess to someone. At least they hadn't said they were worried.

Her job with Crook, the man from the pub, was just another load of crap to add to her already crappy life. Sex with strangers? It didn't seem to matter anymore. Opening her legs and mouth for punters…if it got her cocaine and booze, she'd do it. Crook had given her the money to pay off her debts, and she'd done that, although she'd lied about the amount she needed so she had a stash of alcohol money spare. In her more lucid moments, she acknowledged she'd gone to the dogs, had become a desperate cow who'd do whatever it took to feed her habit.

Life had no meaning, her morals no longer existed, just her need for drugs and drink. What would that old man from the fountain think of her now? He'd been right, she had *been one pay cheque from it all going wrong. If it hadn't been for Crook, she didn't know where she'd be now. She hadn't visited her parents for far too long, although they hadn't phoned to see how she was so likely didn't care.*

No biggie.

Chapter Eighteen

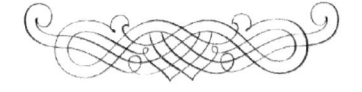

George, now in his forensic suit, had sent Debbie and Nessa away to enjoy the rest of the afternoon. He'd asked them to visit a spa he and Greg wanted to buy as a business front, then give him feedback later, letting him know if it was a decent enough concern for them to get their hands on. An hour or three spent eating and chatting had bitten a chunk out of the day — it was coming up to two o'clock now—and he was ready for action.

He wasn't in the mood to draw the pain out using his medieval tools and had opted to fuck about with these two while they were still in the chairs, then untie Marlborough and hoist her onto the spiked wall rack. One of Mad George's foulest ideas yet had surged into his head as he'd been putting his outfit on, and while it hadn't been Marlborough who'd killed that baby, he wanted to make her understand what Pippa must have felt like when giving birth to a child she knew would never live. Chesney could watch, imagining the pain, and then he'd feel some of his own, the little scrote.

George slapped the cricket stump on his gloved palm and allowed Mad to take over. He glanced at Greg to let him know which side of him had come for a visit. Greg nodded, and instead of standing back to let Mad do his thing, he moved closer in order to stop things if they got too out of hand.

The nugget of Just George who remained, settled, felt safer that his brother had his back. He hadn't told Greg of his plans, so the punishment may never happen once it became clear what

Mad intended to do. Greg's idea of a fun torture session didn't match any of George's personalities.

"Do you even care about what you've done?" Mad asked mother and son, taking the cloths out of their mouths and throwing them on the floor. "I don't see any remorse from either of you, just the fear that you're going to cop it. That means, fundamentally, you're selfish, only bothered about you. Yet you should be bothered about the baby and keeping that woman hostage."

"It was my fault," Chesney said.

"No, it was mine," his mother blurted.

Greg stepped even closer, his eyebrows hiked up. "That's surprised me. I thought you'd blame your son again. Maybe our little chat in the bathroom shamed you into being a good mother. Because you haven't been a good one up until now if you've let him work with you. Now, *our* mother, she hated what we did, she told us we shouldn't do it, which is what decent mums would do, but you? Fuck me, you're a different breed, you are."

"Dickie wanted him in the firm," she said, as though that made it all right.

"Oh, so what Dickie wanted, he got, is that it?" Greg crossed his arms.

"Pretty much."

Mad reminded Just George that their mum had done the same with Ron Cardigan, obeying him even though she knew it wasn't right—for her *or* her sons. Dickie was, well, a dick, always wanting things his own way, so it wasn't a surprise really that Marlborough had done whatever he wanted. The same could be said for Dickie's wife. She'd stayed married to him, even though he'd been playing away. It spoke of the hold he'd had over people. Pippa had also been conditioned to follow a man's rules, obeying Crook, and Just George would never get over how men could treat women that way.

Chesney shook his head. "I swear to you, *I* pushed Pippa. *I* made her lose that baby."

"We know," Mad said. "She told us everything."

Marlborough paled, as if it had hit her even more that they'd fucked up. The fact Pippa had opened up to George and Greg would be galling her. She'd be sick to her stomach that whatever threats she'd issued had been ignored. She must have watched Dickie over the years, picked up pointers, but George had found that even if you tried to act hard, unless it was inside you from the beginning, or beaten into you, you had no chance of pulling it off. Marlborough may have scared Pippa, but that poor girl had faced bigger threats—at least in her mind—with Crook, so this woman here, with her snotty nose and watering eyes, hadn't been someone Pippa had cowered from.

"But she might have made stuff up," Chesney bleated. "What else did she say?"

Mad's anger fizzled, spreading through him, tingling the tips of his toes and fingers. He was close to losing his shit. "We don't need to know anything more than that you pushed her, chained her up, and took her baby to the church. Oh, and you killed a priest and a woman to keep your secret safe. Panic, did you?"

Chesney blushed. "Dublin told the police a woman brought the baby to him—I mean, what an utter div. He was supposed to keep it quiet that he'd seen anyone. I warned him, I told him not to say anything."

Mad chuckled. "Do you think that a scrawny, no-mark kid is going to scare a grown man? Who do you think you are? Dickie?"

"I threatened him. He shit himself."

"Maybe he did at the time, but he obviously thought about it and decided to give the police something to go on in the end. All right, it was lies, but he tried."

Chesney pouted. "He nicked the funeral money."

Mad paused at that. "Was that the guilt talking? Did you want to pay for the funeral because you felt bad?"

"He needed a funeral. He can't get into Heaven otherwise."

Mad eyed him. Did this kid really believe that? George had convinced himself there was a Heaven so his mother wasn't completely gone, but to think you wouldn't get there if you didn't have a funeral was stupid. Wasn't it?

He thought about all the people he'd killed and dumped in the Thames. Where were they, wandering round as lost souls, ghosts?

Nah.

"What are you on?" Mad asked—he didn't want to commend the kid for wanting to give the baby a good sendoff, but fuck it, he admired him for it. At least it meant he had *some* remorse.

Josephine sighed. "We went to that church every Sunday while he was a child. Chesney knows committing that kind of sin is wrong. He just wanted to make amends for the accident."

Mad barked out laughter. "You what? Accident? Fuck off! And you went to church every Sunday, did you? Practised the faith? What a load of old bollocks. Let me see how many commandments you've broken." He took his phone out and Googled. "Here we go. Thou shalt not have no other gods before me—you put Dickie on a pedestal, *he* was your god, so you royally fucked up there. Thou shalt not bear false witness against thy neighbour—the pair of you have said the other one did it, but one of you is lying. Thou shalt not commit adultery." He stared at Marlborough. "You've been seeing Dickie on the side for years while he was still married to his wife. Sorry, but that's not a very Christian thing to do, is it. Thou shalt not kill." He paused to give Chesney a filthy look. "You murdered a baby and two other people—innocents who didn't deserve it, all because you couldn't control yourself. Thou shalt not steal—you ran a drug business under our noses and didn't ask for permission or pay protection money, so to me it's stealing because you kept what wasn't yours. You're not Christians. You're the work of the fucking Devil."

Mad grinned at Greg, pleased with himself for that last sentence.

Greg rolled his eyes then scowled: *Get your head back in the game, you twazzock.*

Yeah, his twin was right. Again.

Mad centred himself. Rolled his shoulders. Drew the cricket stump back and whacked it against Marlborough's ruined cheek. The strike opened up the crust that had formed, and translucent yellow fluid trickled down to her jawline. She gritted her teeth; she must have strong willpower to be able to hold in a scream. Maybe Dickie thumped her once in a while and she was used to it, knew how to keep her emotions in check.

"Who broke your nose?" Mad asked. "Because from where I'm standing, that looks fucked."

"Crook," she said.

Mad's interest piqued. "When was that?"

"This morning. He came for Pippa."

Mad turned to Greg: *Fucking bastard's not going to give up until he finds her.*

Greg returned the stare: *Then get a fucking move on so we can round him up.*

Mad stalked to the end of the table where he'd shifted all the tools while they'd eaten. He selected a jagged-edged hunting knife, admiring the gleam of the steel beneath the harsh lighting, and stood in front of Chesney who squeaked out in protest.

"What do you have to say for yourself?" Mad demanded. "You had an addict come to your office, and while I understand she can't have gear for free, you got arsey and pushed her around. Why? How come you didn't just tell her to fuck off and march her outside? She's young, hardly a threat when it comes to fighting, so there was no reason for you to bully her."

"She went for my mum."

Ah, now *that* Mad could understand.

Chesney continued. "She wound me up. Going on and on, and it pissed me off. I lost it, couldn't control myself."

"Dickie would be well arsey if he were here. He'd say you were a prick, call you all the names under the sun. He'd be *ashamed* of you."

Chesney's eyes filled. "I just wanted to be like him. To be what he wanted. Nessa, she wasn't a boy, so all the pressure was put on me. Dad wouldn't let up, said I needed to step up and prove myself before he publicly admitted I was his."

"You failed him. I bet that stings."

Just George felt sorry for Chesney—but only a bit. Being expected to be someone you weren't, to prove yourself to the one person you craved affection and validation from… And he was only eighteen, one foot still in the quagmire of childhood. He wasn't ready to become a gangster. It wasn't *in* him like it had been for George and Greg. For a start, despite having Mum's softer influence, they'd been brought up living in fear, hatred in their hearts for Richard and Ron, two fathers who hadn't deserved the title. They'd had to become tough little bastards in order to survive. Chesney had clearly been brought up differently. Coddled by his mother.

Mad bent over and put the point of the knife at the top of Chesney's cheekbone. He pushed it in, waited for the lad's wince of pain, then dragged the blade down to his jaw in a slow slice. The skin gaped, showing teeth and gums, and blood, lots of it.

Chesney reared his head, the movement sending his chair backwards. It landed on the floor, claret spraying from the wound. Mad got down on his knees beside him and carved the other cheek, Chesney wailing, crying, and pleading for Mad to stop. Mad ignored him, hacking the end of the dickhead's nose off.

"I've cut off your nose to spite your face," Mad said, "just like you did."

Chesney blinked, uncomprehending, struggling to regulate his breathing. His eyes watered, tears meandering into the cheek slices. "W-what?"

"Greg, look it up so you can explain it." Mad glanced at Marlborough. "Didn't you teach this kid anything?"

She closed her eyes, blocking him out.

Greg walked over. "The phrase means to do something because you're angry, even if it'll cause trouble for you."

Josephine snorted. "So cutting my son's nose off will give *you* trouble?" she asked Mad.

"Only marginally. Our copper will be miffed I fucked with his face for the fun of it. Nothing I can't handle." He addressed Chesney. "*Now* do you get it?"

Chesney nodded. "I didn't think. I—"

"And that's the problem" Mad said. "You didn't think." He looked up at Greg. "We were right to get rid of Dickie when we took over Cardigan. If this is the result of him bringing his son up, he was nothing but a liability."

"My dad was the best," Chesney whimpered between taking huge breaths and choking on blood. Each time he coughed, droplets scattered.

"I don't think so, my old son." Mad rose and pulled Chesney's chair upright. He got right in his face. "If he was, you wouldn't have turned out like this, would you." To Greg, he said, "Time for her to go on the rack."

Marlborough let out a loud screech—it sounded like anger, and Mad vowed to turn that into howls of pain. No way would she be able to hold back any screams with what he was about to do to her.

"Shut your face, you stupid bitch," Mad snarled and took the knife back to the table. He dragged the stepladder to the rack.

Greg untied Marlborough and manhandled her over to the wall. Mad helped him hoist her up then climbed on the ladder to secure one of her wrists. He moved the ladder over to her other side to do the same and, on the top rung, his face close to hers, he smelled the stench of fear coming off her. Greg secured her ankles in place so her legs were spread.

Mad stared at her. "Even if this hadn't happened, you two would have crashed and burned without Dickie. Did you *really* think Nessa would join your ranks? Seriously? When she has a nice little business going on with the Noodle? When she hated her father?" He smiled at the terror in the woman's eyes. "*We* killed your precious bloke. He wasn't even in that coffin — bricks were. There was no car accident."

He enjoyed the moment things slotted into place for her. Not being allowed to see the body, the excuse being he was too bashed up to be recognisable.

"No," she whispered. "I don't believe you."

"Didn't you think it was weird how all his mates went missing at the same time? All those wives asking where their old men had gone?"

"I just thought…I thought a job had gone wrong and they'd left London."

"The power of rumours, eh? And a job *did* go wrong. They tried to rob us, drugs and guns, but Nessa grassed on her own father. She's ours, she's one of us, and you were stupid to think she'd be anything else. You deserve to be here for what you've done. If he'd gone to full term, that baby might have been born addicted, but with help, he could have lived a good life. Instead, he's in a fucking fridge while the police try to find who killed him. And they *will* find you, you and your pathetic son, we'll make sure of it."

He got down off the ladder and returned to the table. Picked up a long-bladed chisel and stood in front of her.

"Did you give birth without pain relief?" he asked.

She shook her head. "Please…no…"

"Then you'll have no idea what Pippa went through, will you. But you're about to find out."

He rammed the chisel upwards into the one place a tool shouldn't go. Her scream started off loud and ended in silence, her mouth an 'O', her eyes scrunched shut, her cracking-open burns streaming fluid. Blood dripped from between her legs onto the floor, and Mad stared at it, the droplets landing with starburst patterns around the edges, a blood spatter analyst's wet dream. He waited for Greg to step in and tell him he'd gone too far, but his brother remained beside him, arms folded, as if to tell Marlborough she had this coming to her. An eye for an eye.

Mad spun to face Chesney. "Got nothing to say, sunshine?"

The lad, transfixed by his mother's agony, seemed to have gone into a daze, although he shook all over, his teeth chattering.

"I *said*, got nothing to say?" Mad shouted.

Chesney snapped out of it and darted his eyes to Greg—he must instinctually know he was the softer out of the two of them, but he received short shrift with Greg ignoring him.

"Don't look at *him* for help," Mad said. "If he hasn't stepped in to stop me now, I doubt he will." He turned back round. Now, instead of droplets, the blood ran like piss—unless Marlborough was actually wetting herself. "I think I've broken something inside you. Shame."

He left her to bleed and took the chisel to a bucket of bleach water he'd prepared earlier. Dropped it inside along with the knife. Picked up some garden shears, snapped them open and shut a few times, and went back to Chesney. "This won't be quite the same as what Pippa and your mother went through, but you'll get the idea." He sighed. "I'm actually bored of cutting cocks off, but how else will you understand?" He opened the blades and settled Chesney's wilted penis between them. "I'll be quick, but it'll still fucking hurt."

"Not my cock. Please, please…"

"Shut your mush, cunt-muffin."

Mad snipped, laughing at the dick tumbling between Chesney's legs to plop on the floor. Blood gushed, creating a stream that spread out and down his inner thighs in rivulets, to pool on the exposed triangle of seat then cascading off, a mini waterfall, splashing on the floor. Chesney screamed, desperately trying to free his arms, his head thrown back, his neck striped with bulging veins. Mad tutted in contempt and strutted off to put the shears in the bucket. He selected a corkscrew and twisted it into Chesney's belly, repeating it over and over in different places, recreating the contractions Pippa would have experienced. Blood pissed out, and Chesney paused for long enough to look down.

He fainted.

"Wimp." Mad walked over to Marlborough. "How does it feel to see your son hurt like that?"

"It wasn't him, it was me… I'm the one you should be hurting. Please, just let him go."

"Liar." Mad inspected between her legs. "The blood's slowing. Bit disappointing. I was willing to watch you bleed to death. Maybe I ought to ram that chisel up your minge again."

Hyperventilating, Marlborough wrenched at the wrist manacles, chafing her skin, muttering incoherently. Mad would bet the rack spikes were doing a number on her back and arse, jabbing her, reminding her where she was and who she'd crossed. Good.

At the table, he put the corkscrew in the bucket and chose his battery-powered blowtorch. Fired that fucker up and burnt the woman's groin area in the region of her womb. What Janine would think about that he didn't know — nor did he care, he was too far gone to give an actual fuck. The police could make of it what they would.

The skin bubbled, like pork scratchings, and yellow-tinged blisters ballooned. He popped one for shits and giggles, wrenching at it and ripping downwards. Burnt the exposed flesh. He didn't know if she screamed or not, too engrossed in what he was doing, only white noise rushing into his ears. He concentrated the heat on her belly button. The flesh, on the cusp of turning black, fascinated him. A charred burger on a barbecue.

"Enough," Greg shouted, his voice penetrating the white noise, creating a hole in Mad's void and allowing Marlborough's scream to invade. "Oi, I said *enough*, bruv."

Only the hand on his shoulder brought Mad out of his trance, and he stepped back, breathing heavily, releasing the blowtorch's ON button. Just George crept in at the edges, an attempt to overtake Mad without riling him. Mad let him flood in. Panting, George stared at what he'd done. Laughed. Didn't regret it for an instant.

"You're a savage bastard sometimes," Greg said. "I was worried for a minute there that I'd have to pull you off, and you know I'm not meant to do anything strenuous yet."

He referred to his almost healed bullet wound, and it dragged George into worry mode.

"Shit. Shit, sorry." George looked into his twin's eyes. "Why did you let me do that to her? The chisel."

"Because I knew why you were doing it. And she deserved it. Come on, get it over and done with. Kill the pair of them and clean them up."

George climbed the ladder and, taking the flick-knife Greg held up, sliced Marlborough's throat. Her neck parted, blood pouring out in a sheet, cascading over her tits and down her wrecked stomach. It lost momentum, stalled by her pubic hairs, drifting through it slowly to then form another piss-like stream below. George watched it for a while, mesmerised, calculating how much of the red stuff she'd lost and how much would be left in her body by the time it had coagulated.

He forced himself out of his reverie and got down. Went to Chesney and contemplated waking him up so the twat would know what was coming. But Greg had said to get a move on, and as much as George would have liked to watch the light of life disappear from Chesney's eyes, his twin's needs were more important.

He swept the blade across Chesney's throat, and for a split second, the kid woke, eyes so wide the tops and bottoms of the whites were visible. He gargled on blood, then his eyes closed, his head dropping back, stretching the wound open.

They got to work laying the pair of them out. It was uncanny how much Chesney resembled his father, albeit a slimmer version. Dickie's face had been weathered, not by the elements but the harshness of his profession, what he'd seen and done over the years giving his features a hard edge. George didn't believe Chesney would have reached that level even if Dickie had remained alive to train him up. The lessons would have been wasted on him.

In the bathroom, George attached the hose to the tap, the one their crew used to clean the warehouse after kills. He sluiced the bodies down. The reason for washing them? He didn't want forensics to take an age working out that the blood wouldn't just be theirs. That someone else's was on their skin once he'd put it there.

At the clinic, he'd paid one of the nurses to take two vials of Pippa's blood — if Janine wanted proper proof these two had a hand in killing that baby, then she'd bloody well get it. He poured it onto their chests, in their hair, and, while it dried, he bagged up their clothing ready to burn at home later.

Greg passed the minutes by sitting on the sofa and playing on the Xbox.

George checked the time. It was technically still too light out to dump the bodies, but if he picked an out-of-the-way spot, they should be all right. The van had an electrician's decal on the side, one they'd peel off after placing the corpses, and, as always, they carried plenty of fake number plates in the back. With stick-on beards as well as sunglasses, they could be any number of bad men around here.

He changed into a new forensic suit in case anyone from the other warehouses happened to be outside. Couldn't risk them seeing the blood. He tossed one to Greg. Outside, he backed the van close to their building, opening the back doors to form shields either side. Plastic sheeting laid out inside the van, he carried the bodies one by one and laid them on top—no way would he let Greg help him, not when he was recuperating. He covered them with an old blanket and locked them inside.

In the warehouse, he studied the blood on the floor. Next time they came here with Crook and Gopher, it would all be gone, magicked away by the crew.

A quick message to them, and he tapped Greg on the shoulder. "Time to go, bruv."

Chapter Nineteen

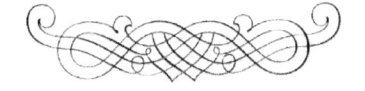

At four o'clock, the sky, overcast in readiness for the coming storm, spread a grey hue over the crime scene. Janine had received the heads-up from the twins on her burner phone but hadn't been able to do anything about it until the official call had come in at the station. One of them, most likely George, had phoned in using a Scottish accent, stating the baby killers had been found and dumped. That call had been traced to a pay-as-you-go throwaway phone, purchased in Ealing four months ago, that had been switched off as soon as the communication had ended. It had pinged the mast in the West End, far from where the bodies were.

The Brothers certainly knew their stuff.

SOCO, in the process of putting a tent up, hurried before the rain lashed down. The forensic manager stood over to the left, instructing someone to do something or other, pointing at the path they stood on. Maybe a piece of evidence had been dropped, or perhaps specks of blood dotted the cream-coloured concrete. People in white suits got on with their jobs, working diligently.

Janine visually processed the scene. The Brothers had been clever—again, most likely George—and had chosen a spot behind a row of boarded-up houses on the edge of a housing estate that was going to the dogs. Minimal risk of them being seen. The homes, once rented to tenants by the council, had a tired air about them, the old-fashioned style showing proof of why they were going to be torn down. Janine envisaged them riddled with damp—she was sure that's what it had said on the news. Beyond the back of the houses, fields that led to another housing estate, which was too far away for any of the residents to see two men putting dead people in the back garden of one of the empty homes. The council were set to knock down half of this estate and build towards the other one, joining the two together.

Tent erected, Janine and the others stepped inside.

She'd forgotten to ask George and Greg to leave a note to make her life easier, but it obviously hadn't slipped *their* minds—one had been placed beside the male's body. It seemed they'd even got Ichabod, their casino manager, to write it, the same as what had been done in the past. This gave her an idea, and she voiced it in front of Colin, Jim, and the forensic scene manager today, Isabella. Their usual, Sheila Sutton, was off on annual leave, visiting her niece, Becky, and Becky's son, Noah.

"Do you think we've got a vigilante out there?" Janine watched each of their faces for reactions to gauge whether they'd gathered yet that whoever left those notes was the same person.

"What," Isabella said, "someone going round finding all the people we can't? I suppose that's possible."

Jim nodded to the note in a sandwich bag which rested beside the male victim's outer thigh, held down with a small chunk of cement, perhaps taken from a pile of rubble a few metres away. "Same writing as the ones we've found before. Whoever it is has been busy on the lookout this past week if the wording is anything to go by on who the victims are. Bang goes my theory on why Luke was left at the church."

Janine read the note. HERE ARE YOUR BABY KILLERS. JUSTICE FOR LUKE!

Thank God it was common knowledge in the press that Jim had named the baby, otherwise there would be grumblings about a leak in the team. Mind you, there was *still* a leak anyway as someone would have told a reporter.

Jim used a pair of tongs to pick the bag up and check the other side of the paper. "Ah, that explains the blood on their chests when there are no wounds there." He held the bag up so they could see.

MOTHER'S BLOOD FOR A DNA TEST TO MATCH IT TO LUKE. YOU'RE WELCOME.

Isabella, stepping forward, appeared eager to swab their chests to get that blood down to the lab immediately, but Jim raised a hand.

"Photos first, please. I shouldn't really have picked this up yet." He put the bag back down where he'd found it.

The photographer came in, a big burly fella, and the tent appeared smaller, more cramped. Janine moved out of the way into a corner, Colin following suit. Janine gave the bodies her full attention. George hadn't said who they were, but she recognised their rings.

"I know them," she said, thankful she had an excuse to say that.

"How the fuck can you?" Colin said. "Look at the state of their faces."

"It's their rings. They're distinctive and they match. That tends to stick in the memory. Josephine Marlborough and Chesney Feathers, Dickie Feathers' mistress and son."

"How come you know them?" Colin asked.

"I remember pulling Dickie over for erratic driving one night. I wasn't even on duty. Those two were in the car with him. Must have been a couple of years ago now. Dickie also had the same ring. He's not long been cremated, he died in a car accident, funny enough, so whoever's left behind in this family will be getting another blow when they're informed of these deaths."

"I'll ring the station to chase up the next of kin." Colin left the tent.

"Why would these two want to kill a baby, though?" Jim mused.

"No idea, but we'll dig into them and see what they got up to."

Isabella blew out a breath, her mask inflating. "Have the lab results come back from the tests done on Luke regarding getting a DNA hit? Sorry, I forgot to check that."

Janine nodded. "Yes. No familial matches on the system, so whoever the mother and father are, they're not criminals, or if they are, they've never been arrested."

Janine didn't want any matches cropping up. The twins had stressed they were dealing with Luke's mum. George and Greg wouldn't have risked the mum's identity being discovered when they planned to stick her in rehab and get her clean. They'd be in protective mode, hiding her from all of this, and wouldn't want her identity confirmed. To do that, they must know she hadn't been arrested and charged for her DNA to be kept on file. The blood left on these bodies would do nothing but confirm she was Luke's mother.

Janine folded her arms. "So we'll continue to try and find her. Not much else we can do, is there." *And it'll come to a dead end every time.*

Jim waved to the departing photographer and stepped up to Josephine. "If this hadn't happened, I'd have stuck by my theory that it was teenagers who panicked when early labour started. Now, with the word 'killer' in the mix on that note, it suggests the baby was murdered. I repeat, why would these two want to get rid of a baby? I'm struggling to get my head around it. Without having Luke's mother around for tests to be done on her, we don't know whether this was a home abortion gone wrong or if labour started by itself. This has kept me up nights, thinking about the various scenarios."

Janine sighed. "Now we know who the killers are, maybe the mother is a family member. We'll soon work it out if she is."

Colin popped his head back in. "I've got the address of the dead woman's sister. Their parents are deceased, no other siblings."

"Okay." Janine stared at Chesney's cheeks. "Those cuts on his face don't look right to me."

Jim cleared his throat. "Serrated knife, that's why. Not the same as what was used on his private parts. Straight, sharp blades down below, possibly large scissors. Could the missing penis be a message? That he's Luke's father, and if it wasn't for him putting it where he shouldn't, none of this would be happening? Do we have an angry dad here—Luke's mum's—who found out this lad here got her pregnant?"

"Possibly." Janine would get the real story from the twins later.

She hung around while Jim did his thing—she needed to find that gun used on Dublin and Hazel. She'd already casually browsed the scene when she'd arrived and hadn't seen it. Jim turned Josephine onto her side. No gun, but she had marks on her back and arse. Familiar ones. Little holes.

"We've seen these before," Jim said. "And, like before, I'll state I think this is caused by some kind of torture device, so the vigilante thing makes sense. Someone who terrorises people to get information out of them. Could this be The

Brothers? They're rumoured to be into that sort of thing."

Janine shook her head. "I doubt it. From what I can gather, that's all it is, rumours. Chinese whispers. They're too into their businesses to be bothered with this lark. The casino, the pub, a hairdresser's, amongst other things."

"You seem to know a lot about how they make their money," Isabella said.

Her snide tone got Janine's back up. "It's my job. If anyone's murdered, despite me thinking it's a load of old tosh that they've done it, I have to bear them in mind. I can go and ask them for their alibi, it's not a problem. They've always been polite whenever I've had to ask for one before."

Jim grunted. "They'll have a watertight one."

"I can still ask for the record."

It was painful, standing there frustrated, unable to tell Jim to get a move on—and get him away from talk about the twins.

After a couple of minutes, he'd finished inspecting Josephine and checked beneath Chesney. "Oh. A gun and another note."

Janine's heart raced. "What does that one say?"

"Err, this has just got interesting. It says: *Gun used at St Matthew's. Male killed them and the baby.* Does that mean the priest and the woman were murdered because Dublin told the police who'd dropped Luke off?"

"No idea, but it's linked, I reckon." Elated that the twins had tied up any loose ends for her, Janine resisted dancing. For now, she had to be serious and play the game, so she took photos of the rings to show the NOK later. "What do you think was used to burn her face and stomach? They don't look the same kind of burn to me."

"From experience, I'd say boiling water on the face and some kind of blowtorch on the abdomen. As you can see, it was held pretty close to the body as this patch here has charred. It's up to you to discover what the significance is. She has marks where she was bound—wrists and ankles. Again, we've seen those before. As for the blood on their chests… It's been poured there for our benefit."

Janine agreed. "Right, well, going back to the gun, here's hoping the striations match the bullets used at the church. We'll go off and speak to the sister, see if she can shed any light on this."

"Let me know," Jim said.

And she knew why. If there was a solid reason for Luke's death, he could make some sense out of it instead of his thoughts constantly churning. Maybe he could then put it to bed.

Janine didn't think she'd be so lucky. Luke had wormed his way into her heart, and she'd remember him until the day she died.

Katy Marlborough wiped her face with a pink, wrinkled tissue. She sat at a table in the break room at her work, having identified the rings as belonging to the deceased. She'd said they were commissioned by Dickie, the only three created to his design, and there was no doubt in Katy's mind that they were the correct ones. She also said the shape of the fingers were the same as her family members', and that Chesney's thumbnail was splayed from when he'd dropped something heavy on it as a child. Basically, this was as close to a formal identification as Janine could get until DNA tests were done.

Colin stood by the closed door to stop anyone from coming in. Several of Katy's colleagues had loitered when Janine had held up her ID and asked to speak to her privately. She wouldn't be surprised if some of them were outside that door now, earwigging. The open-plan office had given Janine no option but to approach Katy in full view, and she imagined them all gossiping now, suspecting Katy of wrongdoing.

Janine had sat opposite her. The news had been delivered, and Katy had finished sobbing, although one wrong word from Janine, and the floodgates could open again. She'd have to be careful, but how could she when she hadn't given the worst of the news yet?

"If I could just get confirmation of what was said." Janine smoothed her trousers over her knees. "That you believe those rings and hands belong to Josephine Marlborough and Chesney Feathers."

"Yes."

"I hate to ask you questions when you've had such awful news, but there's more to come, I'm afraid." Janine drank some tea Colin had made them all. She grimaced — cheap teabags, specks of leaves floating on top, and that horrible red-top milk that may as well be water.

Katy sniffed and dabbed at her red-ended nose. Her eyes, just as red, appeared sore. "What could be worse than telling me my sister and nephew are dead?"

Oh, it can get much worse… "A note was left at the scene which indicated Josephine and Chesney had something to do with the abandoned baby left at the church."

Katy stared. "W-what? I mean, *what*? How is that possible? What did they do?"

"We have no proof, but did they tell you they were involved?"

"No!"

"Do you know whether they were in contact with a pregnant woman?"

"No! No one in our family is expecting a baby." Katy thought for a moment. "Unless…unless Chesney had a girlfriend they didn't tell me about."

"Is that something they'd keep quiet?"

"I'd like to think not. We shared a lot, almost everything. Or I thought we did."

Hmm, I bet they've kept shedloads from you, love. "What did Josephine do for a living?"

Katy picked at the tissue. "She helped Dickie in his office. As a secretary. She's always good at organising things."

"And what about Chesney? Did he have a job?"

"He helped there, too."

"Doing what?"

"I'm not really sure. Maybe he was a driver or something?"

She's being vague. Unless she really doesn't have a clue. "What was the nature of the business?"

"Exports, so Dickie said, but I don't know what they dealt in. Maybe antiques? Josephine has a lot of them at her house, so that makes sense. She only started collecting them when she met Dickie."

"Do you know where the office is?"

Katy shook her head.

Janine pushed on, going in harder. "To your knowledge, have your sister or nephew ever been in possession of a gun?"

Katy's mouth dropped open. "What? No! Why would they need one of *those*?"

"A firearm was found beneath Chesney's body, plus another note. It stated that the gun was used, by Chesney, to murder the priest and his assistant."

Katy blinked rapidly, tears bulging. "This is all too much." She took a few deep breaths. "I don't understand. This isn't like them at all. They'd *never* do anything like this."

"I hate to say it, but they could have been keeping things from you. It certainly looks like that, doesn't it? Josephine was Dickie's mistress after all, so she was used to doing things behind people's backs. He wasn't known for walking on the right side of the law, so the gun could have been his."

"I know he wasn't the most honest of people at one time, but he stopped all that when the twins took over. He went into retirement, got on the straight and narrow."

Janine didn't feel she was going to get anywhere here. Katy clearly believed whatever she'd been told, and no amount of 'making her see' was going to work. If she needed to believe her sister and nephew hadn't been up to no good, then she could for the time being. The investigation would prove otherwise, and when presented with the facts, Katy would have a rude awakening.

Janine smiled. "We'll leave it there for now. If you think of something that might be relevant with regards to the baby, or anything else, please contact me." She took a card out and laid it on the table.

They left the room, two women jumping back to make room, guilty expressions. Janine tutted at them and strode through the large office, eyes following her all the way. Outside by the car, she inhaled a deep breath. Colin got in the passenger side and opened a can of Pepsi Max, so she held two fingers up to him to indicate she needed a break, then wandered along the parking area and got hold of the twins using the burner.

"Thanks for leaving the note," she said to whoever had answered. "It's made my life easier."

"We aim to please." George. "What's up?"

"Can you at least give me the mother's first name so if I come across it, I'll know not to follow that lead? If you don't want her found, I'll have to stop my lot from doing that somehow."

"Pippa someone or other."

"Thank you…"

"I can feel a 'but' coming on."

"Hmm. I've got nothing on why Josephine and Chesney did this. How am I supposed to link them to the mother with fuck all to go on?"

"They ran a drug den," George said and gave her the address.

"How the chuff am I meant to have figured that out?"

"Use your brain. Word on the street, that sort of thing."

"Colin's in the car. It's not like someone could come up to me and give me that sort of info without him seeing, is it."

"Where are you?"

"At the building where Josephine's sister works."

"Then go back inside on your own, visit the loo or something, and come back out saying some bird or other approached you with the info. Later down the line, you realise you forgot to ask her name because you were so excited about getting to the drug office. Things can be simple if you don't overthink it."

"How did you know I was overthinking?"

"Because I know you. Now fuck off and do what I said."

The line went dead, and she checked the burner was on vibrate only, then entered the building. Colin wouldn't follow, the lazy sod. She nipped to the toilets, glad the receptionist wasn't behind her desk to query what she was up to, then hung around in a cubicle for a couple of minutes. When enough time had passed, she legged it to the car and jumped in.

"What's the rush?" Colin asked.

"We've got a lead."

"What lead?"

Janine clicked her seat belt in place and sped off. "Dickie sold drugs from his office, it wasn't exports. A woman inside just told me where it is."

"How did *she* know?" Colin put his can in the cup holder and secured his safety belt.

"She bought from him occasionally."

"What's her name?"

"Fuck it, I forgot to ask. I'm just grateful she was kind enough to come forward with that information. Nobody needs to know who she is anyway. She uses for recreational purposes, so she's no one we need to poke into."

"So she says…"

"Colin, this is the break we've needed. If we can link Luke's mother to the drug office, then we have more chance of finding her, getting her any medical help she may need. Dickie might have kept a tally—if there are names, we'll locate all of them and ask questions."

"Fair enough, but you should have got the informant's name. Just saying."

"I hate that expression. It stinks of smugness."

"Soz."

They arrived at the office, and Janine leapt out of the car. Two vehicles were outside. Would the fibres on the checked blanket match the carpet in one of the boots? George had sent a message to say the cars belonged to Josephine and Chesney and that Nessa had the keys.

Janine found new gloves and booties in a box on the back seat and slipped them on. At the office door, she turned the handle, shocked when it opened, although *should* she be shocked when the twins had likely sent someone to make sure she could get in? She stepped inside and scoped the place out. It looked like any other office with the usual furniture, but one or two things stood out. Scratches on the radiator pipe as if metal had scuffed against it. A kettle on the floor. Some blood.

Colin came in. "Shall I ring Isabella to get another team organised?"

"Please. Call it in to the station an' all. I want to know whose name is on the deeds or tenancy agreement for this place."

And they'd need to go and speak to Dickie's wife. She might know more than Josephine had. His daughter, Nessa, too.

Janine opened a desk drawer and spotted a leather-bound book. She opened it, disappointed to find nicknames instead of proper ones. Dates ran down one side of the page, though, so she flipped through until she got near the back, zeroing in on the days before Luke had been left at the church.

Dog Face – 1 bag – cola.

Chin Scar – 2 bags – thyme.

Barbie – request for sub – denied.

Janine thought back to the dolls that had been around years ago, one her mother had kept. Pippa, a smaller version of a Barbie or Sindy. And it was obvious Barbie was her code name anyway because of the denied sub comment. Cola was coke, thyme for weed? The handwriting was different for a few of the entries—Josephine's and Chesney's? Janine flipped back and found another handwriting style—Dickie's?

She clicked photos of the three versions, planning to ask Dickie's wife later. For now, Janine had to stay here to hand the scene over, so she put her time to good use, poking around while Colin went outside to wait for SOCO and a responding PC. She found a safe, guessing what it contained. Hopefully, if it was drugs and cash, fingerprints would be found on them. While Dickie, Josephine, and Chesney were dead, it would still be good to have proof they'd dealt drugs.

The twins must be livid if they didn't know about this before today.

She stared at the ceiling, thinking about Luke and, very much unlike her, she cried.

Chapter Twenty

The two-year anniversary of Stephanie's murder had come round, the newspapers filled with it as her family campaigned to keep her death in the spotlight. The killers hadn't been found, obviously, and Rod had given a soundbite on the local news, saying he was convinced she'd been killed by someone from St Matthew's. Why was he so sure about that? Maybe someone he'd interviewed had said something to lead him down that path. Not that Pippa wasn't grateful for the misdirection. So long as the investigation didn't swing her way, what did she care?

She'd learned to concentrate only on what she had to do each day.

She stood on the street in Kitchen, blinked, and shook her head. All right, she'd had a skinful before coming out, and she'd snorted some coke Crook had given her, but surely she was seeing things. Someone from her past walked towards her, dolled up and ready for work. Pippa almost didn't recognise her with all that makeup, but the closer she got, the clearer she became.

"What the fuck are you doing here?" Pippa grabbed the woman's arm and dragged her to one side, away from the others. "Are you spying on me? If you think I'm going to say something about what happened, think again. There's no way I'd open my mouth."

Lillibet glanced at the others, then back at Pippa. "I'm not here for that. I start work tonight."

That didn't make sense, and Pippa frowned. "Why? How come you need to do this?"

Lillibet shrugged. "I'm not who you think I am."

"What's that supposed to mean?"

"I don't have rich parents like Fiona and Theresa. I lied my way through that part of my life. I'm in the

shit financially and needed another job. All those fucking expensive clothes and shoes I bought to keep up. You had the same problem, didn't you?"

"Bloody hell... I had no idea we were in the same boat. So how did you get the job? I mean, where did you meet Crook? Because you can't work here unless he says so. If you're not on his books, you'd better find another street to work from."

"Crook offered me the spot when I was down the pub so..."

"But you earned much more than me at Ford's place."

Lillibet shrugged again. "I spent it like water."

"Couldn't you do freelance in the evenings or something?"

"It's in the contract, remember. No moonlighting."

"What about a supermarket job?"

Lillibet laughed. "You're saying this as if you working here is okay but it isn't for me."

"That's because it isn't. I'm no one, I'm a mess. You're worth more than this."

"So are you, yet here you are."

Pippa tugged her away a bit more. "Listen, don't take any drugs if Crook offers them."

"I'm not *that* stupid."

"I was, and look at me. A fucking state. I'm dependent on them. Do the others know what you're doing?"

"No. Fiona left to go and work for a bigger company, so we lost touch. Theresa's gone up the ladder at Ford's now it's expanded, and she keeps to herself. She hasn't been right since...you know."

"Me neither. It's fucked with my head so bad." Pippa's eyes lost focus, and she had to force herself to concentrate. That was the trouble with drink and drugs, they stole your faculties. *"It's the anniversary today."*

"Hmm. I'll never forget it."

"Same."

"I wake up every day, wondering if we'll get caught."

"Me, too." Pippa pushed a strand of hair out of her face. *"Will you just work here for a bit, until you're straight, then leave?"*

"I hope so. Crook, umm, he showed me what I have to do tonight, so I'll be okay, I think."

"By showed you, you mean you had to have sex with him."

Lillibet nodded. *"I thought I'd better do what he said. I need this job."*

"He takes a big cut, you know that, right?"

"Yes, but I'll still be making more than I would in a shop or whatever, plus it's cash, so the taxman won't take a chunk. Anyway…" Lillibet laughed. *"The amount of men I shagged for free whenever we went out, doing this is old hat."*

"But that was different, you chose to go with them."

"And I'm choosing to do it now. Listen, I get what you're saying, but you can't save me—you can't even save yourself. You do you, and I'll do me, all right? We'll look out for each other here, but I have to clear my debts."

"Didn't Crook offer to loan you the money?"

"Yes, but I don't want to owe him. I'd rather pay everyone off bit by bit. I've got a payment plan with them all, so it's fine."

Why hadn't Pippa thought of doing that? "I wish I had. I'll be stuck working for him for years."

"You could come back to Ford's."

"What, you reckon he'd take me back on? I doubt it. I'm too washed up now, fucked in the head. Can't concentrate for shit."

"I'll help you get off the drugs if you like."

"How?"

"I don't know. We'll think of something."

A car drew up, and Lillibet squared her shoulders. "Does he want you or me?"

"You take him." Pippa stepped back. *"I'll wait until you've finished before I go with anyone. We'll take it in turns so one of us is always here. That way, if we don't come back, the other will know."*

Lillibet approached the car. She spoke with the driver, then walked round and opened the passenger-side door. "Wish me luck!"

"Break a leg."

The car zoomed off, and Pippa recalled her first night here, how she'd crapped her pants and cried while the man had fucked her. This job wasn't easy, but she'd got used to it. It was a means to an end, a way to get her precious drink and drugs, nothing more.

She wandered back towards the group, safer by being close to them. Cars came and went, but no one chose her, and she panicked. Was it her appearance? Did she look so manky these days that the men didn't fancy her? She was still young, would have retained her pretty face if she hadn't abused her body, so it was her own fault. Still, as maudlin as she usually was, she'd forever moan about her lot, although she had to admit, while she didn't think Lillibet was suited to this profession, it was *nice to have a friendly face around.*

A vehicle cruised, and Pippa recognised it. What was Gopher doing here again? As Crook's sidekick, he checked the street in person once every night, but he'd already done that, so why was he back? Spying on Lillibet to see how she settled in? He stopped close to Pippa. His window moved down, and he stared straight at her.

"Crook wants a word," he said.

Her stomach rolled over. Had she done something wrong? Had he changed his mind about how much he took off her every night? Panic surged through her, and she gawped at him dumbly, her mind churning over the possibilities.

"Get in the fucking car, then!" he barked.

She snapped out of her head and dashed round the bonnet. In the seat, she stuck her belt on and crossed her arms. She'd never liked Gopher, he spoke to all the girls like they were nothing, and sometimes he looked at her funny.

He drove away.

"What does he want me for?" she asked.

"He doesn't. I lied." His laughter sounded sinister, bouncing around the car.

"What?"

"Shut up, sit still, and do as you're told when we get there."

"Get where?"

"What part of shut up didn't you understand?" He swung his fist to the side and caught her on the nose.

Her eyes watered, and she cuffed the tears away. Why was he being such a wanker? And if Crook didn't want to see her, did he know Gopher had picked her up and was taking her somewhere?

He pulled into an empty car park at the trading estate and switched off the engine. "Get out."

She scrambled from the car, intending to run, but he was right beside her, gripping her arm. He marched her over to a Portakabin next to one of the buildings and wrenched the door open. Had he come here earlier and unlocked it? Or did he rent it? Was it Crook's? He dragged her up the steps then shoved her inside. She staggered forward, hands out, and just managed to stop herself from falling. She stared around. Windows, covered with thick black material, the edges taped to the walls with duct tape. A kitchen area, a few packets of crisps and a carton of milk on the side. A double bed, no sheets, quilt, or pillows, only a bare mattress on a divan base.

"What...what's this?"

"Get on the bed."

"No." She moved towards the door.

He blocked it. "I said, get on the bed."

"No."

He lunged forward, shoving her chest. She stumbled backwards and landed on the mattress. The next second, he was on her, tearing at her clothes. She scratched and fought him, fuelled by the need to get him away from her, but he was too strong. He slapped her face then grabbed her hair, yanking it tight.

"Lie back and take it like you do every night, bitch."

"Get off me."

"Piss off, slut."

He took her then, amid punches and kicks, and she thought of Stephanie, how she must have felt. For the first time, Pippa felt sorry for someone other than herself. But like the old man had said, doing that one good thing wouldn't erase all the bad. It wouldn't take away all the times she'd been selfish, only interested in herself and her feelings.

She had a long way to go before she received redemption, if she even would.

Chapter Twenty-One

Out on yet another search for Pippa, Crook swung round a bend and came to an abrupt halt. Some tosser in gym gear had ignored the lit-up red man on the crossing and waltzed over the road as if he didn't want to live anymore.

"You absolute fucking munter!" Crook shouted, raising his fist to shake it at him.

The bloke flipped him the finger and continued on his way, hefting his Nike holdall into a more comfortable position over his shoulder, laughing. Crook kept meaning to go to the gym, he'd been lax in that department lately, and seeing that bulky pleb only served to rub it in that he'd shirked his routine since Pippa had gone. Another thing to be angry at her for.

Gopher gave Crook a sharp nudge in the ribs. "You should park and go after him. Give him a taste of your fist."

"Yeah, well, I would, but we have more important things to be getting on with."

"You're always staying stuff like that to avoid lumping someone. Are you scared or summat?"

Crook wanted to be a big man but wasn't brave enough to act it when it came to fists. Besides, he could scare people more with his words, not thumps or whatever. He still wouldn't be telling Gopher he didn't like fighting as a form of confrontation, though. He'd get laughed at. The only reason he'd punched Marlborough on the nose was because his temper had got the better of him, and he'd regretted it straight after.

"Scared? Fuck off!" Crook scoffed. "I just think it's better to control people by freaking them out in the head rather than hurting them. A lot can be said for ruling someone just by words. Anyway, if I go around punching people's lights out, I'll have the pigs after me, and that's the last thing we need."

"Fair enough. I prefer dishing out a wallop myself. Gets the point across quicker."

"I know, but you've got to stop that. One day someone's going to report you—and it might not be to the police. We don't want those twins sniffing around. There's too much at stake. Think of all the cash we'd lose if we end up in the nick."

Gopher stared out of the passenger window. "Hmm. I'll admit I've got used to this lifestyle."

"There you go then."

Crook weaved down each street, desperate to see Pippa standing on a corner, his stomach doing flips every time he spotted a woman who resembled her. She had to be making money somehow—he'd got her hooked on drugs, so she'd need cash to buy them, unless she was going cold turkey. But why wasn't she staying at her flat? As far as he knew, she didn't have friends anymore, she'd lost them all, so there was no one to harbour her. Unless one of the other girls had let her kip at theirs. He might have to rethink his stance on violence if he found out they were. Give one of them a punch in front of Gopher so he didn't think he was a wimp.

Road after road produced no sightings, so Crook headed for Pippa's flat. She could actually be inside, hiding out, getting her shopping delivered, not answering the door whenever Lillibet went round there. Maybe she'd applied for benefits, had decided to pack the sex work in, lying low in the hope Crook would forget about her after a while.

Not bloody likely.

He parked outside her block and got out. A quick check of the street, and he was satisfied no one nosed at him. Up the communal garden path and into the shared foyer that stank of dried piss, he waited for Gopher then got in the lift.

"I hate these things," Gopher muttered. "Got stuck in one once when I was a kid. Had to get the fire brigade to sort it out. It had got stuck halfway between floors. It was all right for a while, I suppose, I smoked the fags I'd nicked off my grandad, but I got bored after that."

Crook had listened to many a story from Gopher about his childhood. They couldn't have been brought up more differently. Gopher, always hungry and out to pinch anything he could get his hands on, Crook cosseted and protected, hating it because it meant he couldn't go out and play, let alone experience the thrill of being stuck in a lift. He'd watched film after film about hardmen and had always wanted to be one. Shame he couldn't go the whole hog and batter anyone, though. Maybe if he took up boxing he'd be more inclined to hand out a few knuckle sandwiches here and there.

The lift doors opened, Gopher sighed with relief, and they stepped out. At Pippa's front door, Crook hammered hard with the side of his fist, shouting for her to open up. This was a far cry from when he'd visited her before, picking her up for dates to reel her in. Back then, she'd already been standing there waiting for him.

A bloke came out from next door and peered at him. A brick shithouse. His bald head gleamed from the bulb in the middle of the landing ceiling. "Oi, what's all the fuss about?"

Crook, about to tell the bloke to fuck off until he'd truly clocked the size of him, thought better of it. "Have you seen Pippa? The woman who lives here?"

"Nah. I thought you were her boyfriend, so wouldn't you know?"

Crook didn't like it that the man had noticed him coming here. "I'm worried about her. Haven't seen her for days."

"Me neither. She owes me twenty quid. I should have known I wouldn't get it back, going by the state of her."

Crook frowned. "What do you mean?"

"Drugs, got to be. And booze. She goes to the off-licence up the road to get it about dinner time, comes back with bottles clinking in a bag. Then she sods off out again, pissed as a fart, coming back at all hours, banging about. My mate's seen her in Kitchen Street. Reckons she's a prosser. Good luck trying to get hold of her, because I can't get her to open the fucking door." He went inside, tutting.

Crook looked at Gopher. "How many *other* people does she owe?"

"Chuff knows. I didn't know she was an alchie, though, did you?"

"No. I always thought she was off her tits on coke." Crook whacked the door again. "Pippa, come on now, you've mucked about for long enough." He stepped back. "Kick the door in."

Gopher danced from foot to foot. "Glad you said that."

He shot his foot out, but the door didn't budge. Another two attempts saw it flying open, smacking into the right-hand wall in the hallway. Crook took his flick-knife out, not that he intended to use it, and crept into the poky flat. A horrible thought entered his head, and he sniffed. Nah, if she was dead from an overdose, it'd stink in here.

They checked the rooms and met back in the hallway. Crook stared at the mat. Lillibet was right, there *was* a lot of post.

"She can't have been here for days," Gopher said. "There's washing up in the sink, the plates all crusty. And I'm talking *well* crusty."

"The living room's tidy, same as her bedroom." Crook let out a long breath. "So she's done a proper runner, as in, she's left the East End, maybe even London altogether?"

"Or she's staying with someone we don't know about. I've always said some of the girls probably hide shit from you, but you never listen."

Crook had to accept this may be true, that Pippa hadn't told him everything like he'd thought she had. All those nights he'd dated her, getting her to open up, yet she still may have kept something back. It pissed him off, but a little voice in the back of his head said people were entitled to their privacy.

He hated it when his old self argued with the new one. Bartholemew used to have morals, saw things from both sides of the coin, but where had that got him? People had seen him as a pushover. In some ways, he was similar to Pippa in that he'd tried hard to fit in, to be someone his parents would be proud of, when inside, he was someone else. A selfish prick who wanted money—and lots of it—no matter the cost.

"Fuck this," he said and walked out.

Gopher joined him, closing the door. "You might have to accept the fact she's gone, mate. Put it down to experience. It bears repeating— mark the girls like I told you, cut them so they have a scar that shows they belong to you, or brand the bitches. If you do that, they'll be frightened you might do something worse—they wouldn't dare cross you then. Using words is all well and good until it doesn't work."

"I told Pippa I had connections, that if she ran, I'd still find her."

"Doesn't look like she believed you." Gopher strutted to the lift. "I'm calling it a day. It's pointless searching for her. I'm hungry an' all."

Crook didn't want to go home, so he threw his dog a bone. "We'll go to The Angel for old time's sake. People gossip there. We might hear something. We can have our dinner and a few bevvies, plan what to do next."

Gopher snatched at the bone, like Crook knew he would, his eyes lighting up because free food and booze were on offer.

"If you're paying, then I'm in."

"Of course I'm fucking paying." Crook pressed the lift button. "You're my best mate, and I'll always watch out for you."

Gopher preened. "Good, because if you ever let me down, I'm not fussed about stabbing you, teaching you a lesson, I told you that before. I won't be taken for a mug by anyone, and paying for my own dinner when you've had me traipsing after some slag for days is a bit much."

Crook laughed to cover his nervousness. Jesus, he'd known Gopher had a mean streak underneath his thicko exterior, which was why he'd approached him to be his right-hand man. Crook had needed someone with a bit of beef about him to carry him through, make him look good, be his muscle so he didn't have to do it. For Gopher to remind him he'd think nothing of shanking Crook was unexpected and a bit unsettling, especially as Crook had thought they were good friends now.

Am I getting on his wick, bossing him about?

They stepped onto the lift.

"Sorry, bro." Crook stabbed the button for the ground floor. "I'm getting arsey about her fucking off. Didn't mean to come off as ordering you around. I should have asked if you *wanted* to come to The Angel."

"As it happens I do, but next time, don't treat me like you're my boss."

But I am?

They got off the lift and left the building, Crook reminding himself to watch how he treated Gopher in future. Getting too big for his boots might get him a stab wound if he caught Gopher in a bad mood. The bloke might present as a sandwich short, but Crook had found out he was far from that.

Maybe I should just let her go like he said.

Crook shrugged and got in the car. He might find a new girl in the pub if he got lucky. Chatting her up and dating her would take his mind off Pippa. He'd always enjoyed the entrapment phase.

"Fuck her," he muttered.

He had other fish to fry.

Chapter Twenty-Two

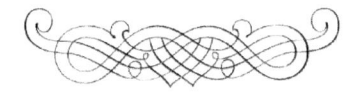

After her relaxing afternoon at the spa, Nessa went to the chippy then round Mum's. She took fish and chips with her—Mum had taken to not eating much since Dickie had died, her way of losing weight. She'd already hinted at trying again with another man, but that wouldn't happen around here. No one in their right mind would take up with Dickie's widow, even if he *was* dead. It was a good job Mum was leaving London, then, starting again elsewhere. No one would know who Dickie was farther afield.

Nessa expected Mum to tell her to fuck off and take a running jump, especially because of how she'd spoken to her when Chesney had arrived at the wake, but the key still turned in the lock, and when she walked into the living room, packing boxes all over the place, Mum smiled at her.

"Wondered when the cat would drag you back in." Mum picked up a drink which may or may not be just lemonade. Her voice had slurred, so it was likely vodka or gin filled that glass. "What do you want?"

Charming as ever. "I brought you dinner, seeing as you've been starving yourself." Nessa handed over a packet of food.

Mum took it, opening it and smiling for once. "You got me cod. Good girl."

The condescension slid off Nessa's back. She sat on the armchair and opened her food. "Sorry about what I said the other day." She wasn't, but there was a reason she didn't want to rock the boat any more than she already had.

Mum waved her apology away. "I've had time to think, and you're right, so don't apologise for telling the truth. I should be the one saying sorry for how I treated you. I'm a cow, and it's about time I faced up to it."

Who is this woman, and who's given my mum a personality transplant? "Oh. I didn't expect that to come out of your mouth."

"No, I don't suppose you did. What Chesney said...it's all been going round and round in my head. I've been a right prat, sticking by your father, staying with him all smug because he never left me for that Marlborough bitch, but I just looked a fool. He went back to her time and again, so I didn't win that game no matter how much I tried to convince myself I did. Him threatening me, making me stay...I *could* have got away if I really wanted. But I didn't. For some warped reason, I *wanted* to stay, and I'll never in a million years understand why. Still, it'll all come out in the wash as my old nan used to say. Marlborough will get what's coming to her. Karma's good like that."

"She's dead," Nessa said bluntly.

Mum paused with a fat, steaming chip halfway to her mouth. "What?"

"Marlborough's dead. It was on the radio on my way over. Her and Chesney were murdered."

Mum's laughter trilled out, and she threw her head back, eyes closed. Nessa ate some fish, waiting for her to calm down. Mum had never laughed much as Nessa had been growing up, she'd been too downtrodden for that, and to hear it now, when it was full of spite...Nessa felt robbed. How nice it would have been to have had a good relationship with her. Going shopping together and all that rubbish. Instead, she'd been shunned, ignored for the most part, until either of her parents wanted to berate her. Nessa was surprised she hadn't grown up fucked in the head.

"Dead? Murdered?" Mum, still holding the chip, broke the tail off her fish, the batter crackling. "That's made my bloody day, that has." She stuffed the tail in her mouth.

"They were dumped behind the houses on Grey Road. Naked. Marlborough had been burnt, and Chesney's face was cut up. Nothing else was said, so maybe the reporters weren't told much else."

"Naked!" Mum laughed again and grabbed her glass. Held it up. "Cheers for dying, you fucking little bitch. I *knew* you'd get your comeuppance in the end."

They ate in silence for a while, Nessa wondering how George had killed them. He'd sent her and Debbie away before he'd got started, and she was glad he hadn't expected her to stick around. On the drive to the spa, Debbie had said being at the warehouse when George went off on one wasn't a pretty sight. Oh, and she'd warned Nessa to say they'd been together all day, the morning spent in Debbie's flat.

Would the twins' copper link all this to Dickie? Desperate for his name to be blackened, Nessa prayed the drug office would be raided and people would know he was a wanker. He'd hate people thinking of him that way, and she hoped he turned in his grave, not that he had one.

Dinner finished, she balled up their chip papers and took them into the kitchen. She dropped them in the bin and put the kettle on to boil. Contemplated Mum's apology, although nothing that woman could say would soften Nessa's heart towards her now. She'd been treated poorly for forty years because she wasn't a boy, and it was her time to like and love herself, to enjoy her life at the Noodle, maybe even find a fella to settle down with.

She'd come here to say sorry for a reason. Mum was leaving everything to Nessa so Chesney couldn't get his hands on it—not that he could now—putting her new house in her name. Nessa was *owed* this, all Dickie's money and assets, for being put through the wringer for all those years. Saying that, she might only end up with whatever house Mum bought once the old bag died. Mum would likely spend all the money living it large now she didn't cower under Dickie's hateful shadow.

It didn't matter, not really. Money couldn't change the past, and spending it wouldn't make it go away either. Nessa would always have her memories, the remnants of hurt that popped up inside her from time to time, but the difference these days was they didn't gouge deep anymore. She'd long accepted that Dickie had despised her, the same for her mother, and it wasn't Nessa's fault she'd been born to selfish, arsehole parents.

Tea made, she walked down the hallway, frowning at two people-shaped figures on the other side of the glass in the front door. She took the cups into the living room, put them on the coffee table, and asked, "Are you expecting anyone?"

Mum frowned. "No, why?"

"There's someone at the door. They haven't knocked yet, which is odd. They're just standing there."

"Go and see who it is then."

"What? It could be anyone!"

Mum tutted. "No one would dare hassle me or try to break in."

"They might now Dickie isn't around."

Mum appeared worried for a second, then got up. "I'll go."

Nessa followed her out into the hallway.

Mum threw the front door open and barked, "What are you doing, loitering about out here? Fuck off before I phone the police on you."

Nessa peered over Mum's shoulder.

The woman held up some ID. "DI Janine Sheldon, and this is my partner, DS Colin Broadly."

Oh shit.

"So? What do you want, a medal?" Mum said.

"Could we have a chat with you inside?" Janine glanced past Mum and clocked Nessa.

"What about?" Mum asked.

"If we could just come in, I'll explain everything."

Mum stood her ground. "If you're here about Dickie, then whatever he did is not my problem, so you can fuck off if you think you're going to pin his shit on me."

"That's not why we're here. As far as I'm aware, you haven't done anything wrong."

Mum huffed. "Okay, but don't get comfy. You won't be staying long."

Still amazed by how her mother had changed from meek and mild to a gobby bitch since Dickie's death, Nessa walked into the living room and sat on the armchair. She picked up her tea for something to occupy her hands and waited for everyone to file in. Mum plonked down on her seat and swigged some of her drink from the glass, then lifted her tea mug and held it on her lap.

"We just boiled the kettle, and it's empty now, so no cuppa for you," Mum said.

"It's fine, we don't want one anyway," Janine said, just as snarky.

Colin raised his eyebrows. "Speak for yourself. I don't mind making my own."

Mum glared at him. "Cheeky bastard. No, you can't make your own, not in this house. Gone are the days when a man makes himself at home here."

That went against her recent admission that she wanted a new fella, and Nessa frowned, putting her cup down as it was burning her fingers.

"Okay, first off," Janine said, "I'll get this out of the way. Where were you today, Mrs Feathers? Specifically this afternoon?"

"Down the Con club with her next door. We went to bingo."

"Who is her next door?"

"*Her*!" Mum jerked a thumb to her right. "Doreen White."

"What time did you arrive?"

"About twelve. We had lunch there, a sandwich and a cream cake. Bingo started at two. We left at five, getting the bus home. I got in here about sixish, then Nessa came."

Janine swivelled her gaze to Nessa. "And you? What were you doing?"

"I went to a spa with Debbie from The Angel."

Janine's eyebrows shot up. "Debbie? Know her well, do you?"

"We both run pubs, so we were comparing notes."

"Which spa was this?"

"The one The Brothers are thinking of buying." Nessa had said that to let Janine know she was on her side—they both worked for the twins, and she hoped Janine would have her back. "It's called Relaxology."

"I know the one. Did you come straight here from there?"

"No, I dropped Debbie at The Angel, then went up the chippy. I came here after that."

Janine wrote that down. "Do either of you recognise this handwriting?" She took her phone out. "There are three styles." She went closer to Mum and showed her, swiping from one to the other.

"That one's Dickie's," Mum said. "No idea who did the others."

Janine let Nessa have a look.

"That's Dad's. I don't have a clue about the other two either."

Janine addressed Mum. "Were you aware your husband had a mistress and a son?"

Mum nodded. "Yes."

"How did you feel about that?"

"Pissed off, as you can imagine. Hurt, upset, but we're talking about Dickie Feathers here, so what the hell could I have done about it? He threatened me, said that if I ever left him because of it, he'd kill me. So I kept quiet, got on with it. Why?"

"Have you seen the news at all?"

"How could I? I was at bingo, then like I said, Nessa turned up with our dinner. Look, what's this about?"

Janine scratched her eyebrow. "Josephine Marlborough and Chesney Feathers were found dead today. They were murdered."

"And?" Mum stared at Janine. "You're telling me this because…?" She slapped the arm of her seat. "Oh, I get it. You want to know where me and my daughter were in case it was us, do you? Well, I may have hated the woman, couldn't bloody stand her, in fact, but I wouldn't stoop so low as to kill her, nor her weirdo kid."

"Do you know of anyone who may have wanted to kill them?" Janine asked.

"Plenty. She was up her own arse, all that going to church business, thinking because she sang hymns of a Sunday she was all that and a dollop of caviar. Well, she may have come across as sweet and innocent, but she was far from it.

Not only was she a husband stealer, but she dealt drugs."

Was it Nessa's imagination, or had Janine done a sneaky fist bump down by her side? What was that all about?

Janine's face didn't betray her gesture. "Do you know where she sold them from?"

"An office Dickie owned. Down Rembrandt Close. Hardly anyone else around, easy for him to do his dodgy dealings without being seen."

"Did you know about this when he was alive?"

"Did I buggery. I found his notebook after he'd copped it. Everything's listed in there. Do you want it?" Mum reached across to the drawer of the nearby bureau and pulled it open. She felt about inside then produced a diary. "Here, you might solve a fair few crimes after looking in there."

Janine took it. "Why didn't you hand this in when you found it?"

Mum sent her a piercing stare. "Just be glad I've given it to you, all right? Now, if you don't mind, my cuppa's going cold." She sipped, ignoring them.

Nessa stood. "I'll show you out."

She followed Janine and Colin to the door. Colin bustled off to a car and got in. Nessa went outside and closed the door to.

On the path, Janine whispered, "You already knew, didn't you? Before it hit the news?"

"Depends. Say I helped the twins today. Would you accept that I was with Debbie all morning in her flat at The Angel, then we went to the spa?"

"So long as Debbie says the same thing, yes. So my records match."

"Then yes, I already knew. I was the one who took Pippa to Moon's clinic."

"Is she okay?"

"She will be."

"What the hell happened for it to come to this?"

"Ask the twins." Nessa walked inside and closed the door. Leaned on it.

Jesus Christ, she needed whatever Mum had been drinking. A large one.

Chapter Twenty-Three

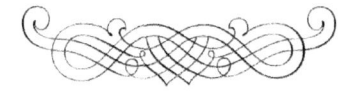

The word PREGNANT on the pee stick came as a bit of a shock. Pippa's periods had been all over the place before she'd had the contraceptive injection, and they'd all but stopped after she'd had it, so not seeing blood down there had become the norm. But she'd forgotten to get a new jab and had only realised that months after Gopher had raped her. She'd been experiencing sore breasts, and her tummy had swollen.

She'd put it down to the drink, but at the flutter of movement in her abdomen, the horrible truth had slammed into her mind.

What was she going to do? Crook wouldn't let her work if she was up the duff, and she didn't even want a kid. She sat in her flat and counted backwards, working out a rough estimate of how far gone she was. Googled to see if a termination was on the cards.

No, she was too far along.

Shit.

In a panic, she rushed outside to walk to Kitchen Street. She needed to speak to Lillibet, get some advice, because surely the baby inside her would be ruined, considering what she put in her body on the daily. Maybe, if she took extra cocaine and drank a whole bottle of neat vodka, it would kill it. That would solve all of her problems. Did she feel guilty for thinking that way? No. She could barely look after herself, let alone a child. She could give it up for adoption, though. But that didn't solve everything — how could she disguise her bump in the coming months? Crook would spot it, but maybe, if she was lucky, he'd beat the shit out of her and she'd lose it. That wouldn't be her fault, then. She could shirk any responsibility.

She reached Kitchen and went straight to Lillibet, drawing her away so they could speak privately.

"What the fuck's up with you?" Lillibet asked. "You look awful. Sorry, but you do. Worse than usual."

Pippa moved close to Lillibet's ear and whispered, "I'm sodding pregnant."

Lillibet drew back, her eyes wide. "How far gone?"

"Too far to get rid of it."

"Oh God. Is it a punter's?"

"No. You know that night you first started, and I said I'd wait for you. The reason I didn't was because Gopher came. He took me to this Portakabin and...well, you can fill in the blanks."

"Did you give him permission?"

"No."

"Oh my God. Oh Jesus. Does Crook know?"

"I didn't say anything because I doubt he'd believe me over Gopher."

"But that was ages ago. How come you've only just found out?"

Pippa explained about the injection. "I was in a really bad place then, my mind all over the place, which is why I forgot to get another one."

"What are you going to do?"

"Try and get rid if it myself."

"How?"

"I don't know. Maybe I should get on the brown, overdose and be done with it."

"Don't say that."

"Well, it's not like I have the best life, is it. I never have."

"Feeling sorry for yourself won't help."

"What else is there?" The familiar black cloud cloaked Pippa, and she had the urge to punch herself in the stomach. Why did bad shit always happen to her? What had she done in a previous life to deserve this? Why hadn't she taken the old man's advice and changed her outlook, been a nicer person? If she had, maybe she wouldn't be in this position now. She'd never have gone out with Lillibet, Theresa, and Fiona. Never have liked the taste of booze and how it made her feel. Never have gone round Stephanie's. Never got herself in so much debt she couldn't see a way out. Never have met Crook or Gopher. And she'd never have had this fucking baby inside her.

"This is a chance to make amends for what we did," Lillibet said. *"You can get clean, have the baby. It'll be a focus, someone else to love and care for. You can sort yourself out. How long before you've finished paying Crook back?"*

"Ages."

"How long is ages?"

"Too long, all right?"

"Fuck. Can't you get a day job so you can pay him back quicker?"

"We've had this conversation before. I'm in too much of a state for anyone to employ me."

"We'll have a chat tomorrow. I'll come round yours. There's got to be a way out of this."

"I'll give it up, I don't want kids, but how will I get away with working here in the meantime? The bump's going to get bigger."

"It's not very big now, considering how many months you are, so maybe it won't grow too much more. If you can just hide it from Crook and Gopher until you've had it. Maybe say, when you've given birth, that you're ill so you've got time to hand the baby over to whoever."

"Do you think that'll work? Really?"

"It doesn't look like you have much choice, does it."

Chapter Twenty-Four

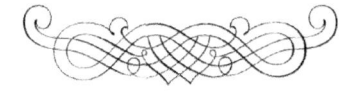

Debbie stood behind the bar at The Angel, keeping an eye on Crook and Gopher who sat at the back in a booth. A server took their food trays away, and the two men supped on pints of lager, their third, talking with their heads close together. What were they plotting? Ways to find Pippa? Debbie had already messaged the twins to let them know their targets were in residence, so now all she had to do was keep them in her sights until George and Greg arrived.

Which would have been great if Janine and her sidekick hadn't just walked in.

What the fuck does she want? Don't say the twins have sent her to arrest those two.

"What can I get you? Vodka? Bacardi?" Debbie asked. "Or is this an official visit?"

The bloke with her—was his name Colin? Debbie wasn't completely sure—sniffed the air and eyed an elderly married couple nearby who ate their dinner.

"I should be doing that," he grumbled. He licked his lips and scowled at Janine. "Instead, we're doing overtime."

Janine plucked a menu off the bar and handed it to him. "Stop moaning and go and get a table. Message your wife to tell her you'll stop by the Chinese on the way home and get her dinner. We'll eat here, okay?"

"I'm not paying these prices," Colin said. "It's cheaper down the Noodle, *and* they've got fancier food."

"Oi," Debbie said. "You can always turn round and walk back out again. No one's forcing you to eat my grub." She'd have to look at her overheads and see if she could lower her prices. People might stop coming here now the twins' pub had become well-known for being value for money. Or she'd have a word with George and Greg, tell them they were fucking with her business.

Janine cut in. "I'll buy it, Col."

He handed the menu back, smiling. "I'll have the pie and mash. Steak and kidney. Oh, and some of that liquor gravy. And mushy peas."

Janine gave him a nudge. "Lovely, now bugger off."

Colin ambled away, sitting in the booth next to Crook and Gopher.

Janine smiled at Debbie. "I'll have the fish and chips, and that man over there by the door will have the same. Thanks."

The bodyguard Debbie had heard about. She prodded the buttons on the till to order their food. "Cameron?"

"Yes."

Debbie totalled it up, opened the till drawer, then closed it again. "On the house. What drinks would you like?"

"Three Cokes, please, just in case we have to go back to work after this. I hope the free meal isn't a bribe."

Debbie laughed. "We both know I don't have to bribe you." As she poured the drinks, she checked the corner booth. "Just a heads-up, so you may want to turn the other cheek. Those two in the corner, in the booth next to Colin—that's his name isn't it?"

Janine nodded.

"Well, the twins are coming to *collect* them."

Janine lifted her head in acknowledgment. "Okay. I'll sit with my back to the pub, then. If they happen to come in behind me, I won't see them, will I. Or I could nip to the loo if you give me the nod. Colin won't do anything, he's retiring and can never be arsed to get involved if he doesn't have to."

"I'm not sure if they're coming in the front or the back."

"Bugger. Changing the subject..." Janine moved closer. "Just for my records, can you confirm what you've been doing all day?"

Debbie put two Cokes on the bar and poured the last one, saying quietly, "I was with Nessa Feathers from the Noodle. We were in my flat this morning, then we went to Relaxology, a spa, this afternoon."

"Thanks. That's the official story, all right?"

"Yep. So you've heard, then? About the mother and son? Stupid question. Everyone's heard, it was on the news. People have been yakking on about it in here ever since."

"Hmm, we were at the scene earlier." Janine sipped one of the Cokes.

"Is it bad?"

"As bad as can be expected when it comes to you know who."

Debbie whispered, "Her face was already fucked when I saw it, before they'd got anywhere near her. Pippa did it to get away from her."

"I'm still not sure of the full story, a certain person we know and love was being awkward about giving me information, but I'll ask them when they have a free moment. I knew they were going after Crook, so I expect I'll be updated after he's been dealt with."

"It's all very sad."

"You're telling me. Seeing that baby…" Janine took the black plastic tray Debbie gave her and put the three Cokes on top. "I spoke to Nessa not long ago. She said Pippa is as okay as she can be." She looked over at Colin. "He doesn't know I'm aware of who she is, by the way."

"I gathered that. Anyway, I've said as much as I can so…"

"Yep." Janine walked to Colin, placing the tray on the table.

The bodyguard strode over there and sat with them. Were Janine and Cameron an item? He certainly sat close to her, or was that a ruse in front of Colin to disguise the fact he followed her around all day? Debbie decided she didn't really give a shit and served someone else. At the end of pulling the pint, she gave away yet another drink because her burner vibrated in her pocket and she needed to check it. She went to the other end of the bar where no customers stood and read the message.

GG: GET THEM IN THE PARLOUR.

DEBBIE: WILL DO.

GG: WE'RE IN YOUR OLD ROOM.

DEBBIE: GOT IT.

She lifted the bar hatch and wandered towards the corner booth. Crook glanced up at her approach, and a scowl appeared.

"Hi, sorry to bother you," she said, "but we're currently running freebies in the massage parlour to drum up repeat custom. Your table number came out in today's draw. Are you interested?"

Crook looked at Janine then back to Debbie. "*Shh*. She's a copper."

"So?" Debbie said. "We're only offering you a massage." She rounded her eyes to let him know there was more on offer than that.

He got the gist and nodded, then turned to Gopher. "Are you okay with that?"

"All right, don't mind if we do."

Debbie smiled. "If you'd come this way…"

She guided them towards the double doors and pushed through, holding one open for the men. She took a left through another doorway that opened onto a corridor that led to the parlour. At a third door, she peered up at the security camera and rang the bell. The buzzer sounded, and she showed the men into reception.

Crook gazed around at the expensive red carpet, black leather sofas, and a couple of oak coffee tables. Soft music played from the stereo on top of a matching sideboard beside a fake potted plant—she used to have real ones but kept forgetting to water them, so she'd had them replaced. Crook appeared impressed and seemed to take mental notes. What was he planning, to run his own parlour?

That may be his dream at the minute, but in a few more, he'd realise he wouldn't be able to do anything of the sort.

"If you'd like to take a seat." She gestured to the sofas. "Someone will be ready for you soon. Would you like to be seen separately, or are you happy for two women to see to you both at the same time?"

Gopher whooped, an alarming sound, and slapped Crook on the back. "A foursome. You up for that?"

Crook blushed, appearing uncomfortable, but he nodded. "No touching me, though. I'm not into men."

"Like I would." Gopher flopped onto a sofa and stretched his legs out.

Crook sat opposite, his back ramrod straight. How could a man who ran girls act so out of his depth? She'd known him as Bartholemew, who'd drunk his pints on his own and failed at chatting up the ladies. He'd changed, though, and when she'd heard he now called himself Crook, she'd had trouble holding in laughter. She could spot a novice a mile away, and he was it.

She walked over to the desk, sitting beside Amaryllis who shouldn't still be here. "Um, where's Belladonna?"

"She's running late. Sam's got the lurgy."

Debbie felt sorry for Belladonna's son, he was a good kid. "Aww, what kind?"

"Stomach bug. I don't mind staying on. She's waiting for Lottie to get back from the chemist with something or other for him."

Belladonna and Lottie had been married to the same man without knowing it. With their husband, Mack, out of the way, they'd formed a combined family of sorts, the children from each marriage getting to know their half-siblings, the wives finding common ground and becoming friends.

"How long will she be?" Debbie asked.

"About half an hour."

"Good." Debbie leaned close and whispered, "As you've probably gathered, those two are being picked up."

"Ah, I did wonder." Amaryllis pressed the intercom for Debbie's old room. "Your customers are here, girls."

"Send them through."

Debbie almost burst out laughing at one of the twins faking a woman's voice. She went back over to Crook and Gopher. "They're ready for you now." She led them to her door and opened it. Stared in.

No one was in sight.

The men walked inside, and she shut the door, ignoring the instant sounds of a scuffle, a thump or two, and swearing from George, the main word being cockwomble.

Debbie rolled her eyes at Amaryllis. "All in a day's work, eh?"

Amaryllis grinned. "Fancy a cuppa?"

Chapter Twenty-Five

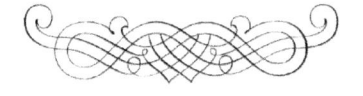

Crook and Gopher sat tied to the chairs at the warehouse. George waited for Mad to make an appearance, but it seemed his nutty side didn't want to come out to play any more today. Neither did Ruffian. Tired, Just George wanted to nip to the Taj with Greg for some grub then go home and chill. They *could* leave the men here, drugged up to their eyeballs, and ask Martin to babysit, but George didn't fancy facing this crap tomorrow. Best to get it over and done with.

And Debbie had messaged, a rant about food prices, so he'd said they'd meet her at the Indian as soon as they could. She clearly had a bee in her bonnet, so to save Moon getting on their arses once he got back from abroad, they'd speak to her and come to some kind of agreement with whatever the hell it was.

Some days just went on and on with no end in sight.

In yet another forensic suit, he paced in front of their quarry. Greg played a game on the sofa. He'd complained of feeling tired, breathless, and George had instructed him to rest. Greg had headphones on, and maybe he was too tired to give much of a fuck about being there to stop his twin if he went too far. Perhaps he *wanted* George to cross the line, considering what these two had done. Maybe Greg had a little Mad inside him, too, since he'd got shot.

It had been a long, emotional day. So much going on. Too many feelings to suppress while they'd gone about their business. It took a toll.

"So, explain what the fuck you think you're doing, luring women in, getting them hooked on drugs, and forcing them to sell their bodies for you. That's some next-level bollocks, that is, and to say I'm not best pleased is an understatement."

Crook widened his eyes, the image of innocence. "What? Who told you *that* rubbish?"

George sighed. Really? They were playing *that* game? "Don't act dumb with me, moron. You run girls in Kitchen Street. Pippa told us everything."

"That fucking slag," Gopher muttered. "I *told* you not to trust her. There was something about her that wasn't right. Didn't I say that? Eh?"

"Shut up," Crook snapped. "It was my decision, my outfit, but I hold my hands up, I got it wrong with her, all right?"

George slapped Crook round the head. "When you two fannies have *quite* finished… Answer my question. What were you playing at?"

"Look, I didn't think I had to tell you, okay?" Crook said, a hint of belligerence in his tone.

"How many times have I heard that before as a cop-out? I know this is a big estate and not everyone knows the rules, but for people like you there's a grapevine, and I don't believe you were oblivious."

Crook tilted his chin. "What do I owe you? That's what this is about, isn't it? You want all that protection money I didn't pay? I can get it for you. Just say how much, and it's yours."

George sneered. "At one time it would have been about the money and you not running this by me and my brother first, but now it's a different matter altogether. See, because you got Pippa hooked on drugs, she had to find her coke from somewhere. She found Josephine Marlborough and Chesney Feathers, and a few days ago, when she was desperate—and without money, probably because you took it all off her—she went to them, begging for a sub. Chesney got arsey about it, pushed her, and she fell."

"So?" Gopher said.

"Shut your fucking mouth," George roared. He calmed himself. "I'll come to you in a minute." He retuned his attention to Crook. "She landed on her stomach. She was pregnant, did you know that?"

Crook appeared shocked. "Bloody hell. I *told* her to use condoms. You were there when I said it, Goph, so back me up here, will you? I'm not fucking lying, George. I don't want my girls full of disease, passing it to everyone they service. I've got a rep to maintain."

"Oh, she did use protection—when she was allowed."

Crook frowned. "What's *that* supposed to mean?"

George jerked his head at Gopher. "Why don't you ask your mate there?"

Gopher paled, his eyelid twitching. "Don't bring me into it. I don't pay anyone for sex."

George took a step forward. "No, you just take it, don't you. You rape women instead."

Crook stared at Gopher, incomprehension furrowing his brow. "Is this true?"

Gopher tutted. "What are you listening to *him* for? You know Pippa's probably told him a load of old blarney so he does exactly what he's doing. Think about it. With us dead, she doesn't have to pay you back anymore. Jesus, use your loaf, will you?"

Disgusted by Gopher, George said to him, "I'm willing to bet, if I took your blood and gave it to the police, it'd be a familial match to Luke, the baby who was found in the church."

Crook's mouth hung open. "You what? That kid was *yours*? Fucking hell, it's been all over the news and you didn't tell me nothing."

"He's the father," George said. "Your pal *raped* one of your women."

"No. No, he wouldn't do that."

George gritted his teeth. "I imagine you've been trying to find Pippa because you're losing money every day she isn't on Kitchen. Want to know where she's been? I'll tell you. Chained up in Marlborough's office. She was supposed to be killed, but the person who was asked to do it came to us instead. Because of you, Pippa got herself into a mess and lost her kid."

Crook wagged his head from side to side. "I…I didn't know he was the dad, I swear."

"So you admit you knew she was pregnant?"

"No! I didn't have a clue. Jesus, do you think I'd let her carry on taking drugs if she was? I'm not a fucking monster."

"That's debateable," George said. "I mean, you were willing to send her out there to get shagged by any Tom, Dick, or Harry, and that's okay by you, but the fact she was up the duff makes a difference? Tell me how your mind works, how that first scenario is all right when the women don't want to be sex workers. Explain it to me."

"Okay, I'll admit it, they don't want to be at first, but I persuade them, then they're fine about it."

"By persuade, you mean threaten to kill them or their family, yes?"

Crook dropped his chin to his chest. "I wanted to be someone, okay? A face. That's all."

"So did Chesney. All you pricks are the same. You want to be a face but lack the nous to carry it off. You want all the riches but have no idea how to treat the people you deal with. Fucking scum, the pair of you." George took a deep breath. "So let's talk about the rest of the story. Chesney, he takes the baby to the church and warns the priest to keep his gob shut. The priest did that for a while, then caved when he got a visit from the pigs again. He said a woman had dropped the baby off. Chesney found out. Have you been watching the news lately?"

Crook shrugged. "Been busy an' that."

"Right. Well, the priest got killed, as did some poor cow, all because of you and what you started. Those deaths are on your hands, their blood is, even though Chesney did it. And now Marlborough and Chesney are dead—*I* fucking killed them today—and here we are."

"Why is it my fault?" Crook asked. "Jesus. I helped Pippa, I paid off her debts—or I gave her the money so she could do it. If she didn't, that's on her. She had to work for me to pay it off. What's wrong with that? I bet you do similar, don't you?"

"We run things in a fair way. The only time we get nasty... Why the fuck am I explaining myself to you? You could have taken monthly repayments without drawing her towards drugs and putting her on Kitchen. You didn't need to be such an arsehole about it."

"It's the only way. She'd have fucked me about each month if I didn't give her rules."

George shook his head. "Rules? You're not getting it, are you?"

"I don't see the problem, no."

"I'm wasting my fucking time..." George whipped his gun out and pressed the business end to Crook's forehead. "Maybe *this* will make you see the light."

Crook pissed himself, his jeans going dark at the crotch. "Please, I didn't mean for any of this to happen. I never hurt them, I didn't touch any of them, didn't hit them or nothing."

"No, but you fucked with their heads, didn't you."

"Yeah, but… Aww, come on, can we work this out? I'm *sorry*, okay? I'll tell the girls they can go. They don't have to work for me anymore."

"No, because they'll be working for Debbie."

Crook closed his eyes. Opened them.

George pulled the trigger.

Blood and brain shot out. George wished he stood behind him so it could spray on his face. He hadn't had that happen for a while.

He moved to stand in front of Gopher.

The man paled even more and squirmed. "What he's done is fuck all to do with me."

"But you didn't stop it, did you. You let him carry on treating those women like shit. You took what wasn't yours with Pippa. She said no, yet you carried on, laughing in her face while you were at it. You're fucking disgusting, do you know that?"

"She needed teaching a lesson in how to fuck. Men had been complaining."

"So raping her taught her what? How to be afraid? You're warped in the bastard head, son."

"I'm not your son."

"No, you're not, and thank fuck for that. I'd be ashamed of you if you were."

Gopher seemed to cotton on to the gravity of the situation. "My mum…"

"What about her?"

"Will you tell her I love her?"

"Nope. I couldn't give two shits about passing on any messages for you. Not after what you've done."

"Will she know I'm dead?"

"I haven't considered her, seeing as I've had arseholes to deal with all day. Maybe she'll be told what happened and to keep her mouth shut, maybe she won't. I don't know her so can't judge whether she's likely to listen to our words of warning. Some people don't, you know. They go tattling to other leaders, but it doesn't do them any good. We get told, and they end up dead. Your old dear might be the type to go to the police and grass us up. In that case, I'd rather just let her wonder whether you'll ever come home again."

"She's a good sort. She'll not tell anyone."

George didn't believe this wanker. "Nah, I think I'll keep your ending to myself." He shot him in the forehead and, turning away, sent a message up to Luke. "There you go, littlun. All sorted by Uncle George. Now go and find my mum. She'll look after you."

At the back of the Taj at their usual out-of-the-way table, George and Greg sat opposite Debbie who'd brought Nessa along. It was just as well, they could all get on the same page, as with Nessa here, the rant about the food prices suddenly made sense.

George didn't let her know he knew that, though. "So what's the issue, Deb?"

"Janine came in The Angel." Debbie raised her hand to shut him up. "I'll tell you why in a minute. Colin, the bloke she works with, moaned about my food prices and said he'd be better off going to the Noodle. No offence or anything, but for fuck's sake, what if everyone decided to do that? How can I keep The Angel going if every man and his dog sods off to your pub instead?"

"I can see your point." George speared a piece of chicken. "Either lower yours to be competitive or work out how much you're losing. I'll take it on the chin and make up the difference. But if your takings went down before the Noodle got up and running, then that's not our problem."

"I've looked, and they took a nosedive the week after your place opened. Only the food, though."

"Fair enough. How much are you losing a week?"

"About eight hundred, and even though I thought about it, I've decided I don't want your handouts."

George considered that. "All right, what about getting your food from our suppliers? They're cheap, so you can lower your prices. I'll send you their number."

Debbie nodded. "Fine. But if I'm still working at a loss, we'll talk again."

George played devil's advocate. "What would you have done if the Noodle wasn't ours? Would you have gone to the landlord and had a go at him?"

"Of course not."

"So why rave at me?"

Debbie flushed. "Hmm, put like that, it makes me look a cow."

George smiled. "Always happy to hold up a mirror. So, what did Janine want?"

"She'd come in to ask for my alibi, make sure it matches Nessa's. She's going with the version that we were in my flat all morning then went to the spa."

Nessa scooped rice up. She'd only asked for a small meal as she'd had McDonald's for lunch and a chippy tea today. "She came to my mum's, too."

Greg ripped a naan in half. "Makes sense, what with Marlborough and Chesney copping it. She has to be seen as going through the motions."

Nessa sipped her wine. "She asked where we'd been. Mum was at bingo, so she couldn't be accused. I told Janine to ask you for any details. I wasn't sure how much you tell her."

George nodded. "Cheers. We'll have a word with her tomorrow. I can't be arsed now. I'm too tired to deal with her, especially as she'll rip me a new one about the state of the bodies. So, thoughts on the spa?"

Debbie leaned her elbow on the table and poked her fork towards him. "If you're going to go there in your size tens, not advisable. You'd have no customers left. The people we saw were the Zen crowd, they go there to relax, not get worried. Other than that, it seems a decent going concern. Why is the owner selling?"

George smirked. "They're not."

Nessa frowned. "So how can you... Ah, I get it. You're going to *persuade* them to sell."

"Got it in one."

"Why do you even want a spa on your books?" Debbie asked.

"High-end clientele. Men who might want a massage elsewhere, if you catch my drift. I can send them to the parlour at The Angel. And there will be people who want recreational drugs. And a therapist, so Vic would benefit. And then there's Under the Dryer. Custom is always welcome there, and people always need haircuts."

"Smart move," Debbie said.

"They don't call me Brain Box for nothing."

"Since when has anyone called you *that*?" Debbie scoffed.

"Bog off." George glanced at Greg who'd barely spoken. "You all right, bruv?"

Greg shrugged. "I will be once we get home."

They ate and chatted, George sensing they had a real ally in Nessa now. He was still a bit pissed off with her for not telling them she was going to the drug office to start with, but she'd proven herself before by letting them know Dickie and his gang of reprobates were trying to get into Under the Dryer and nick the goods. She'd got her own dad killed, so she was well and truly on their side.

George fished in his pocket and brought out a thick envelope. He dropped it on the table. "That's for you, Nessa."

She stared at it. "What?"

"The money equivalent of the drugs Chesney put in your car when you took his mum to the safe house."

"Oh. Right. Thanks. But why is it mine?"

"We'll be selling the gear, and you were the one to help Pippa, so you deserve it."

"Can you do me one more favour?" she asked.

"What's that?"

"Get word out about Dickie running the drugs, maybe add some rumours that make him look bad. I want his name blackened."

George shrugged. "Fine by me."

The topic turned to Debbie visiting the women on Kitchen Street soon and how she was glad to have a distraction.

She sighed. "I'm going to miss Moon."

"Yeah, he said at the last leader meeting he was doing business abroad. Amsterdam. He didn't say what it was, though."

"I don't know, and even if I did, I'd leave it for him to tell you."

George studied her, how she seemed softer around the edges now. "You really love him, don't you."

Debbie's cheeks turned pinker. "Just a bit."

Nessa sat back, her food all gone. "My dad used to hate him."

Debbie laughed. "Many people do, but he's lovely when you get to know him."

"Salt of the earth," Greg said.

George slapped the table. He didn't want to get into a lovely-dovey conversation about Moon. "So, if we're all square, it's business as usual, all right?" He rose and dropped a wad money on the table along with a large tip. "We're going home, but if you two want a pudding or more drinks, knock yourselves out. There's enough cash there."

Nessa glanced at Debbie who nodded.

"Fuck it, let's get pissed."

George walked out with Greg, smiling.

Looked like Nessa had found herself a friend.

Chapter Twenty-Six

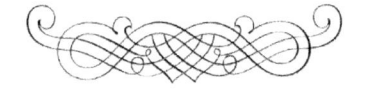

A few days had passed since Pippa had done the test, and she'd had time to think about what to do next. She was going to get some brown, take too much, and end it all. What was the point in being here anyway? No one cared about her—well, maybe Lillibet—and it wasn't like she'd be missed. Crook wouldn't get his money back, but that was the least of her worries. She didn't even have any to pay her

dealers, but she'd been going to them for a long time, so maybe they'd give her a sub? They didn't need to know she wasn't going to be around to pay them back.

She knocked on the door of the office and waited. Miss Marlborough flung it open and smiled, gesturing for Pippa to go in. Marlborough locked the door, which was usual practice, and Pippa went to stand by the kitchen area, nervous as hell.

"What can we get you?" Chesney asked from his seat at the desk.

"I need some brown."

Marlborough raised her eyebrows. She'd be the one to refuse the sub, but Chesney might talk her round.

"Brown?" Marlborough asked. "You're usually a coke girl."

"It's not doing the job." Pippa leaned against one of the kitchen floor cupboards. "It's getting harder and harder to get high."

"If it wasn't for people like you, we wouldn't be in business," Marlborough said, "so me saying this will sound odd, but you shouldn't have got yourself hooked in the first place."

"I had no choice."

"How come?"

"I work for Crook, remember."

"You could still have said no. Taking coke isn't a requirement to being a sex worker."

"No, but… I owe him money, okay?"

"Ah, so you have to do as you're told." *Marlborough looked at her son. "See this? The state of her? If I ever find out you've dipped into the goods, there'll be trouble. You don't touch it, you hear me?"*

"I'm not that dumb." Chesney eyed Pippa. "You know once you go on the brown it's a shit sight harder to get off it, don't you."

Pippa nodded. "I need it."

"What happens when you get yourself even more fucked up?" he asked. "You'll end up on methadone, scratching the shit out of your arms while you stand in the chemist and wait your turn to be given a dose."

"I'm prepared for that." She wasn't, she planned to be dead come the morning.

"Okay, that's the warning chat over." Chesney smiled. "We wouldn't want to just hand over a new drug without letting you know the consequences. As my dad would have said, that wouldn't be ethical."

Like this lot ever are. Fucking Nora. *"I know what I'm doing."*

"Fine." Chesney stood, ready to go over to the safe. "How much do you need?"

"Enough for a few hits so I don't have to come back for a while."

He stared at her. "Do you have any idea how much that will cost?"

Pippa squirmed. "See, here's the thing…"

"Oh dear," Marlborough said. "Please tell me you're not going to ask us to lend it to you. That's not how this works."

"Please, I just need one sub, just one."

"No." Marlborough turned her back and headed for the door.

Fear and anger took over Pippa. She rushed forward and shoved Marlborough's back. The woman lurched forward, breaking her fall with her hands on the door. Chesney leapt up and gripped the tops of Pippa's arms, his eyes blazing.

"Don't you dare touch my mother, you skanky little bitch."

He pushed her, and she careened backwards at speed. He advanced, clearly filled with mania, and snatched at her hair.

"Punch me," she said. "Go on, punch me in the stomach."

"You fucking what?" He dragged her towards the door. "Get out."

She held his arms, staring into his face. "Please, just let me have it. I swear I'll pay you back. I can't do this anymore. I need...I have to..."

He flung her hands off him. "No."

Marlborough had recovered and went to twist the key in the lock to let Pippa out. Pippa slapped Marlborough's hand away, desperation clawing at her. She couldn't have this baby, she couldn't. These two were the only ones who could make it all better. Unless she slit her wrists. Or took paracetamol, but that might not work.

The second push from Chesney came as a shock.

"I said, don't touch my mother."

Pippa went for him, fists up. If they weren't going to sub her, then they could beat the shit out of her, do the job for her. Make her lose the kid. Kill her. She didn't care. Another push sent her to the floor, and she landed on her stomach. She laughed, praying it would do the trick.

"I'm going to phone the coppers on you. You'll be in the shit for dealing drugs." Wetness filled her knickers, and she hoped it was blood or the waters breaking. A ripping pain shot across her abdomen. "Ouch."

"Get up and get out," Chesney ordered.

Pippa got to her feet, and the wetness dripped down her legs.

Chesney stared at it, and he paled. "Oh fuck. Fuck!"

Marlborough sighed. "Look what you've done now." She glared at her son. "She can get us in all kinds of crap over this."

Pippa stared down. Blood dribbled from beneath her short skirt, on her inner thighs, her knees, towards her ankles. Seeing it snapped her into…into what, she didn't know, but suddenly it was real, she was pregnant, and she was losing it. Visible blood brought her reality crashing into her, and she remembered what Lillibet had said. This could be a new start, Pippa could get clean, bring the baby up. Have a focus.

Now it was happening, she didn't want to miscarry. She didn't want to die.

"Help me," she said. "Please…"

"You're pregnant," Marlborough stated. "You're pregnant and you're taking drugs? You absolute piece of filth."

Chesney punched Pippa, and everything went dark.

Chapter Twenty-Seven

The next day, her head muzzy from last night's booze-up with Nessa, Debbie introduced herself to the women on Kitchen Street. She'd asked one of them to contact the night-time girls so she could speak to them all at once. After a half-hour wait, they'd all gathered by a lamppost and stared at her, wary, as if she was off her rocker by coming here to take over

Crook's patch. She supposed it *would* look weird, considering they were used to being ruled by a man who'd threatened them and, in turn, could threaten Debbie for taking over his livelihood. They'd find it hard to trust her, but over time, Debbie hoped to completely win them round.

"Where the fuck's he gone?" someone shouted from the sidelines. "He makes too much money off us to just piss off."

"He's no longer going to be a problem for you," Debbie said, "believe me."

The collective drop of everyone's shoulders told the story well enough. None of them had liked their pimp, and who could blame them?

"Where's he gone, then?" a blonde at the front asked.

Debbie smiled. "Sorry, I didn't catch your name."

"Lillibet. He used to make me spy on everyone, you know, and I hated it. I told them all what I was doing, didn't I, girls? I didn't want them thinking I'd go against them for that wanker."

Debbie admired her honesty. Perhaps these women had formed a family, having each other's backs. "He's *missing*. So is Gopher."

"Missing?" Lillibet, clearly taking on the role of leader, folded her arms over her scantily clad chest. "What sort of missing?"

Debbie took a deep breath. She'd been given the go-ahead to reveal the truth—with a warning for them to keep their mouths shut. "The Brothers' sort, but if any of you blab about it, you'll be in trouble."

"Oh shit," someone at the back whispered. "I bet they're dead."

"How come?" Lillibet flicked her head to toss hair out of her face.

"Unfortunately, Crook messed with the wrong girl, they both did."

"Pippa?" Lillibet asked.

"Yes. She's moving away, so you won't see her around here again, but with your pimp and his sidekick out of the picture, I'm worried about you all. So are the twins. I'm here to make you an offer."

"Like what?" Lillibet stuck a foot out and cocked her other hip.

"You continue to work here, except you keep all of your money bar fifty pounds a week, which comes to me so I can pay the watchers. They will monitor you at all times, the same as on my corner by The Angel. You'll receive burner phones, and we have a system where all number plates are checked. If the drivers come back clean, they have no criminal records, then it's safe to go with them. All punters must agree to being in our database, otherwise they can fuck off. My girls are *never* put in danger."

"What about our regulars, though?" someone said. "Some of them have been coming to us for years and never laid a hand on us. We trust them."

"Even if you're totally sure about them, they go into the system just the same. As for the ones you've got a dodgy feeling about or any newcomers, then they can take a running jump."

"So we have to give you fifty quid a week?" the brunette asked. "Is that all? Where's the catch?"

"There isn't one. I used to be in your shoes, and all I want is to help you work in a secure environment. I know it sounds like it's too good to be true, but I promise you, I'm genuine. Some of you have kids, yes? People who love you? I'll make sure you get home to them at night—I provide free taxis. If you want to speak to any of my girls on my other corner to see if I'm on the level, feel free."

"I've heard good things about you," a black-haired woman in her forties said. "Been wanting a spot on your corner for ages."

"Did you apply?" Debbie asked.

"Nah, didn't think I'd get in. I mean, look at me. I'm considered past my best. You could have told me to fuck off."

Debbie eyed them all one by one. "I had an older woman on my corner, age doesn't matter to me. She's now my daytime receptionist in the parlour. Here's something you need to know, and I say this as advice, not being condescending. If you never try, you'll never get anywhere. If you don't ask, you don't get. There are women who've worked on my corner who went up the ladder into my parlour. There are others who've left the profession altogether and have new careers. If you're looked after by me, then that means the twins look after you, too. If they have spots open for certain jobs, they might pick you. Come on, be braver. Dream big. You don't always have to be a sex worker. If you want to continue in that line of work, no one will judge, but if you don't…"

"I'm in," Black Hair said. "Stupid not to when Crook nabbed most of our money. Fucking hell, I'll be able to afford the electric this winter now."

Others muttered their agreement.

Debbie stared at Lillibet. "What about you?"

Lillibet smiled. "Oh, go on, then."

"Brilliant. How about you become one of my managers here."

Lillibet nodded.

Debbie picked out Black Hair. "And you can run the night-time shift if you want. As well as earning your own money with punters, I'll pay you to be here for everyone and report to me if anything's off."

"Fucking Nora," Black Hair said. "Are you serious?"

"Yes. What's your name?"

"Sharny."

"Okay, is everyone all right with that? Lillibet and Sharny are your go-to people?"

The crowd agreed, and a thrill went through Debbie. She'd had a period of hibernation with Moon, had healed herself, faced her past head-on and told it to piss right off. And now?

She was back in the game.

Chapter Twenty-Eight

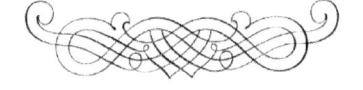

Nessa's head hurt. She hadn't got pissed up like that for a long time, but it had been worth it. She and Debbie had gelled really well, and although some would say two landladies couldn't possibly be friends because of the competition, they'd found themselves comparing notes and laughing uproariously at some of the ridiculous things customers said.

Nessa had enjoyed it so much she'd decided she wouldn't work seven days a week anymore. Debbie had offered for them to go to the spa again, or on other nights out when Moon was busy, and since that meant finding time, Nessa was going to leave the Noodle in her staff's hands sometimes. Susie would be fine taking her place for a few hours.

She pulled a pint of lager for the old duffer, Arthur O'Connor, and handed it over. He paid, moaning that it was a shame the drink prices weren't as cheap as the food, but she smiled regardless. She was only the manager here, the twins were the ones who made the rules, and the grumbling sod was aware of that. Like Dickie, some people loved to naff her off for the sake of it. Shame Arthur had become one of them.

She glanced over at the door as it swung open. Mum breezed in and, thumb poked in the direction of Nessa's private flat door, she walked over there and waited. Nessa sighed. She didn't have it in her for a row today. Still, she led the way upstairs to a door that was always kept locked.

In her flat, she went straight to the kitchen and stuck the kettle on. "Unusual for you to visit me."

Mum sat at the mini breakfast bar. "I've never understood why people have these stools. They're so bloody awkward to sit on."

"Good job you don't live here, then." Nessa took cups out of a cupboard and put teabags in them. "To what do I owe this honour?"

"I've sold the house."

Nessa hadn't expected that so soon. "Oh. That went pretty quick."

"Some weirdo who wants to live in Dickie's house. One of those gangster-loving types, you know the sort."

"Hmm." Nessa couldn't bring herself to be pleased about the sale for anyone but herself. At last, her life would be her own with Mum going up north. "So what happens now?"

"I either look for a house to buy or I rent one. I think I'll rent, though. That way I can get a feel for the town I end up in, see which areas are better. My solicitor's daughter is sorting it all for me. She's my estate agent."

"When do you think you'll be gone by?"

"Hopefully inside a month. Why, will you miss me?"

"Err, no."

Mum laughed, despite the harsh barb. "Can't say I blame you. But oddly, I'll miss you."

"You'll miss having me on hand to do things for you or to pick fault in, more like."

Mum snorted. "Hurry up with that tea. My tongue thinks my lips have been sewn shut."

So that was the end of any sentimentality, then. Good. Nessa didn't want to stand here talking about something neither of them were invested in, like their relationship.

An hour later, Mum packed off home, Nessa returned to the bar. The news had been full of the two recent deaths, a few older gentleman having a chinwag about it. Some customers gave her sympathetic looks, as if losing her father as well as her half-brother had affected her negatively, but they needn't have bothered.

Inside, she was having a party.

Then she sobered. Luke had suffered because of Chesney. Pippa had, too. Being pleased was a bit selfish when others had gone through so much, but hadn't she, too? Her whole life?

"So it says here that the gun used to killed Dublin and Hazel was the one found near the bodies," Arthur said on his bar stool, stabbing his newspaper with a blunt-ended finger. His flat cap was skew-whiff, the grey hair at his temples peeking out. "And the blood on Josephine and Chesney belongs to Luke's mother. What the fuck has gone on?"

"No idea," Nessa said. "I barely knew Chesney or his mum. It's not like they were invited round for Sunday dinner, is it."

"Nah, s'pose not, considering what your old man was up to. I always suspected he was seeing her, right from years ago. Your mum, she kept telling everyone for a while, until Dickie shut her down. That poor cow's well shot of him."

So am I. "Poor cow? She's not as sensitive as she makes out."

Arthur eyed her. "Hmm, I bet she had to be a strong woman to put up with the likes of him."

"Or stupid," Nessa said.

"No love lost there, then?"

"Absolutely not. My parents… D'you know what, I'm not even going to explain. We never got on, end of story."

"But it's never the end, is it. Shit like that stays with you forever."

"Not if I can help it."

"I used to be homeless, you know. Lived on the streets. Pigeons used to come and sit on my shoulder. What I'm saying is, you can't forget that sort of shit, the stuff that hurts you deep."

"I can."

She smiled to herself. Finally, it was her time.

And she was going to love every minute of it.

Chapter Twenty-Nine

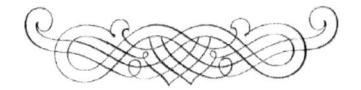

Janine stared down at tiny Luke for the last time on his metal drawer bed. Jim had put a nest of blue blankets beneath him since she'd last been here. The pathologist had a heart of gold, and she worried about him. He appeared haggard, as if sleep was limited. She knew that feeling.

The blood results had come back with a familial match—Pippa was his mother. Now it was looking likely that the CPS would accept the evidence that Marlborough and Chesney had had a hand in Luke's death, the baby's body was being released. The people of the East End and beyond had donated to the funeral costs at the fund-raiser, as had the twins, and so much cash had come rolling in. Someone had made the decision to send the rest to the neonatal unit at the nearest hospital in memory of the miniature boy who'd struggled to take his first breath, if he even had. The funeral was tomorrow, and everyone had agreed to put on bright colours instead of the usual black.

"I wonder if his mum is watching all this on the news," Janine said, guessing Pippa was, but she was unable to say so for obvious reasons.

Jim let out a long sigh. "I wish I knew she was okay. I think about her a lot, you know. I worry whether she's alive, whether she's dead—she could have given birth in an alley, left Luke, and crawled off somewhere to die from blood loss."

"But Dublin said a young woman had dropped him off. That has to be the mother, yes?"

"Let's hope so."

"Entertaining horrible scenarios is only going to make you ill. Please take care of yourself. I don't want you to get poorly and have to give up your job. Sod working with another pathologist."

He laughed gently then sobered. "You know what I get like when it's children. I can cope with adult deaths, but kids, they mess with my mind. This one more than any other."

"I've been having nightmares about it, and Colin hasn't coped very well, so you're not alone."

"It's the mystery of it, the not knowing that's bugging me."

"Maybe we'll never find out who she is. She could be from a family who'd disown her if they found out she'd had a baby. There could be all sorts of reasons why she hasn't come forward. And she must be alive. That blood on Marlborough and Chesney was fresh, remember."

"True. But how did it get on them? Did *she* slice their throats?"

"No, it's the vigilante. There were the wounds on Marlborough's back, the same as we've seen before. How they got the blood from her, I don't know. Maybe the vigilante found her, and she donated it freely." She had to change the subject before Jim delved too deep. She looked down at

Luke. "I won't come back to see him again, not now he's being buried. I expect he'll be off to the undertaker soon."

"He will." Jim sighed. "I bought him a new outfit."

Janine bit her bottom lip. "Don't, you'll set me off."

"Such a tragedy. No one will ever know what he could have been, who he would have become."

"Jim, stop it, all right? You're tormenting yourself." *And me.*

He nodded, weary. "Maybe when we lay him to rest, the hurt will fade."

She smiled sadly. "Maybe."

But she doubted it.

With Cameron sitting in his car beside the play park and Colin doing paperwork at the station, Janine met the twins. They sat at a picnic table amongst some trees, cans of Coke to hand, brought by George.

They'd told her the full story, and now she understood why Pippa needed to be relocated. A new start, to find out who she wanted to be this time, and to put the ordeal behind her. Out of the several jobs George had found for her, she'd chosen an estate up north, and Will was going to drive her there and help her to get settled in once she'd finished rehab. They'd be hiring a van to cart her furniture, and her job was with a man called Jimmy who ran the Barrington Patch.

"It's the funeral tomorrow," she said. "Will Pippa be going?"

George massaged his temples. "With us, yeah."

"I'll be there, as will Colin and others from the station who've been affected by Luke's death. The crowd will be watched, you realise that, don't you."

"Yeah, but there will be hundreds of people there. Pippa won't stand out."

Janine gulped some Coke, wishing it was the diet version. "It'll eventually become a cold-case file. The mother got away, The End."

"Good."

"Anything else I need to be aware of?"

George shook his head. "Nope."

She stood. "See you tomorrow, then."

"We'll ignore you," Greg said.

"Obviously."

Janine strolled away and got in Cameron's car for a quick chat.

"Everything all right, love?" he asked.

She sighed, so bloody tired. "It will be once we get the funeral out of the way. Closure an' all that."

"You got attached to him, didn't you. The baby."

"Hmm."

"Makes me wonder if you want kids of your own deep down."

She side-eyed him in shock. "Err, no."

"Are you sure?"

Janine loved yet hated the way Cameron made her think, getting her to push her own boundaries and tear down the walls she'd erected around herself. "Sod off."

Cameron laughed. "I can read you like a book."

She folded her arms. "Well, this one isn't going to turn into a fairy tale where the couple end up having a sprog, so you can get that out of your head."

"We'll see."

She elbowed him, laughing, and got out, going to her own car. Switching her mind off that scenario so she didn't give it any legs, she returned her mind to the paperwork awaiting her. The shitty instant coffee at the station. Chivvying Colin along to hurry him up. Fielding questions. Updating the DCI.

Her life was full enough, thanks. She didn't need a baby in it. Didn't want to turn out the same as her mother, a useless parent.

She navigated the streets, all the mums pushing prams standing out, like that game people played, spot the yellow car. If you were looking for it, you saw it everywhere. But she *wasn't* looking. She wasn't.

You bloody are.

Chapter Thirty

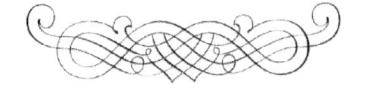

The day didn't dawn wet and dreary, as appropriate for funerals. The sun shone brightly, as if God had welcomed the baby into Heaven and it was a celebration, not a reason for tears. Pippa couldn't get her head around her rehab nurse telling her that to celebrate a life lived, no matter how short, was better for your soul than to sob your heart out. But that nurse wasn't Luke's mother, she didn't have children, and she could never fathom how awful Pippa felt. For not wanting him. For wanting him once she knew she couldn't.

To see the proof of him, his tiny body, had brought it home that no matter whether she'd been raped, she *could* have loved him, even if he'd grown up to look like his father. His features would have become his own eventually, and she'd have learned to love him for who he was, not for who his dad had been.

All of that had been taken away from her by Chesney—and, if she were honest, her own stupid actions in life—so was there any point in lamenting now? Luke was gone, and Pippa had a future to get on with without him. At one time she'd have been glad about that, but sometimes she caught herself imagining pushing his pram, him gurgling at her. There would be no first time smiling, rolling over, sitting, laughing, walking.

And to think she'd likely damaged him with all those drugs she'd taken. And the drink. Had she ignored the fact she'd forgotten to get another jab on purpose? Maybe she'd always known she was pregnant but didn't want to face it, to have to make a decision whether to keep him or have a termination. She had no idea how you went about that sort of thing, nor how it worked.

So many emotions roiled through her that she found it difficult to breathe. Despite her sunglasses, she squinted from the direct sunlight. George put his arm round her and gave her a squeeze, and Greg took her hand in his and gripped it tight. Maybe they'd sensed her inner turmoil and wanted to reassure her that although she'd had those wicked thoughts, it didn't make her a bad person. Except she hadn't told anyone about those thoughts except for Will, and she didn't think for one minute he'd have shared them with the twins. As for Stephanie's murder, that would be a secret she'd take to her grave.

The new priest at St Matthew's, an older gentleman, intoned some words Pippa didn't hear. She blocked them out, because any diatribe about a little lamb being taken into God's arms wouldn't stop her from feeling rotten. Guilty.

Finally, it came time to throw earth on the coffin, but she couldn't do that. It felt wrong somehow, like having mud on it meant Luke was dirty—the product of a filthy, sordid union she hadn't wanted. So she walked away, catching sight of Janine and her sergeant with an older man who cried. George and Greg had said members of the police would be here, but she hadn't expected any of them to show such raw emotion. Maybe he was the pathologist who had named her son. George had said he'd be coming. Apparently, Jim had taken this death badly and worried about Pippa.

The ragged look on the pathologist's face propelled Pippa towards him. Janine stared at her in shock and shook her head slightly, but Pippa ignored it, scoping out her escape route. She spied a pathway between trees, and if she pushed through all the mourners to get to it, anyone following would soon lose sight of her.

She stood beside Jim and held his hand. Whispered, "Thank you for caring for my son."

He whipped his head round to look at her. "What?"

"Luke," she said.

Jim spluttered and stared at Janine as if to tell her she needed to guide Pippa away and take her in for questioning. Janine blinked at him.

"Let her go," she said quietly.

"But..." Jim turned back to Pippa. "What happened?"

"I'll write you a letter," Pippa said. "But I loved him in the end, and I would have loved him more if he'd lived."

She left it at that, weaving through the crowd, Janine's sergeant asking what the chuff was going on because he'd missed that conversation.

"Nothing for you to worry about," Janine said.

Pippa walked on, to the pathway, to that break in the hedges that signified her new life. Will appeared, and he went down it with her, leading her to a bus stop. They'd both been driven here in the twins' BMW.

"Feel better for doing that?" he asked as they sat on a bench to wait for the number seventeen.

"A bit."

Now she had rehab to finish, more time to reflect. After that, she'd become a new person.

"You shouldn't have let her go," Jim muttered. "She needs a checkup to make sure she's okay."

Janine sighed. "She looked fine to me. Stop worrying."

"Won't you get in trouble for just letting her walk off?"

"Not if no one mentions she was here."

Jim seemed to wrestle with that. "I don't know, it's all a bit cloak and dagger to me."

"She doesn't want to be found. And she said she'd write to you. You can give the letter to me after you've read it if you want to, and I'll pop it into evidence. If she reveals what happened, then there might not be any criminal charges to be brought against her."

"But you don't know that, yet you let her go."

"Because I believe Luke's birth was brought about because of Josephine and Chesney."

"But you don't *know* that."

I hope he isn't going to be become a problem. I'd hate for the twins to have to give him a visit. "Did you not see that man she walked off with?"

"I'm not tall enough to see over everyone's heads."

"I bet he's made sure she's been taken care of. I've seen him around, I know where he hangs out, so if it makes you feel better, I'll ask him to put me in touch with her, all right? I'll get a statement off her."

"What if he won't help you?"

"Then he'll be in the shit, won't he." Janine was going to have to insist that Pippa wrote her version of events and sent it in officially. She could leave her name out of it, but as long as Janine had something to get Jim off her back…

I could curse her for fucking this up.

"Let me know how it all goes," Jim said.

Janine gritted her teeth. "Will do."

George had picked up on the exchange between Pippa and Jim. Jesus Christ, *what* had George said to her? Under no circumstances could she speak to anyone. This would royally mess things up for Janine who'd now have to explain things to her DCI if Jim didn't keep his trap shut. She'd have to make an excuse as to why she'd let Pippa walk away.

Maybe she can say she thought the woman was a crank…

Either way, he'd be having words with Pippa.

God, why couldn't things ever be plain sailing?

Chapter Thirty-One

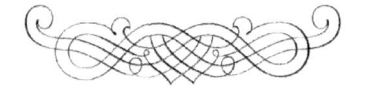

Three Months Later

Pippa had got over the arse-chewing from George and had written to the police and the pathologist to tell her side of the story. Will had stopped halfway up north for her to post the envelopes, and she'd had gloves on while writing, at George's insistence. Will was staying with her for a week until she got settled in.

She sat in the living room of her two-bed rented house on the Barrington Patch, a man called Jimmy sitting opposite—he'd be paying all her bills, plus extra wages on top. He'd gone through what he expected of her, and she'd agreed to his terms. Cassie, the old Barrington leader, would be coming home from abroad for a visit soon, and Pippa would also get to meet her. Apparently, Cassie would give her some pointers on how to do her job effectively.

How odd, to work for a man who was the equivalent of George and Greg, although Jimmy wasn't half as menacing. He reminded her of David Beckham to look at.

"So you think you can handle being a part of the team?" Jimmy asked. "I'll warn you, things aren't pretty sometimes, and you'll be doing things most other women wouldn't."

"If you pay me well, you'll get no complaints." There she went again, thinking money was the be all and end all. Hadn't she learned *anything*?

"The pay's good, so…" Jimmy told her what it was and stood. "I'll see you in the morning, then."

Pippa saw him out then returned to the lounge.

Will eyed her as if he wasn't sure who she was and the woman he knew had fucked off, never to be seen again. "So you don't mind beating people up for a living, then? I wouldn't have put you down as that type."

Pippa squared her shoulders. "I've got a lot of rage inside me. It has to go somewhere. Anyway, this is the job George found for me, so he must have had a reason to suggest it. Maybe he thinks this is my calling."

"What, to become the next Cassie Grafton?"

Pippa shrugged and smiled to hide her trepidation. "Why not?"

Will shook his head. "If you're sure."

She wasn't sure of anything, but if cutting people's faces meant she'd forget what she'd been through, what she'd done, she was all for it. She reached across the sofa to pick Bear up and hugged him, hoping he'd give her comfort in the new life that lay ahead of her.

Chapter Thirty-Two

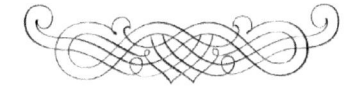

One Month Later

Lillibet stood at a fruit machine in Jackpot Palace, surreptitiously watching the manager, Ichabod, with Katy Marlborough. Katy flirted, it was obvious by her body language, and it seemed Ichabod didn't know how to respond to it. He appeared awkward and somewhat trapped.

Lillibet had grown up in the same road where Katy lived and had often seen Josephine when she'd come to visit her sister. Plus she'd gone to school with Chesney, and while she was older than him by a few years, she'd played with him in the street along with all the other kids. He'd been a weird little git, but she'd felt sorry for him. She didn't now, though. Finding out via the news he'd basically killed Luke, plus the priest and that woman, had shocked and disgusted her. Who'd have thought he'd have done something like *that*?

Katy and Ichabod drifted closer, or it was more like Ichabod tried to get away and Katy followed.

"Why don't you take me out, then," Katy said. "A night on the town away from this place will work wonders if you're down in the dumps."

Ichabod shrugged. "I don't know. I like tae work."

The Irish accent had always charmed Lillibet. It reminded her of her great-uncle.

"Oh, come on. All work and no play makes Ichabod a dull boy," Katy said.

Fuck me, what a shit pickup line.

Lillibet wanted to warn Ichabod that Katy was a bit of a tart. Maybe he knew already and that's why he was trying to wheedle his way out of her suggestion. As the couple's conversation bounced from Katy being persuasive and Ichabod being evasive, Lillibet got bored.

She collected her coat, handing her ticket over, and walked into the foyer. She stared out into Entertainment Plaza at all the people in restaurant windows. The water of the central fountain, lit up with pulses of multicoloured strobes, had streaks of lightning superimposed on it from some kind of projector.

Doing up her coat buttons and drawing her collar up to keep her neck warm, she left the casino and wandered down the left-hand side of the Plaza. If she was lucky she'd pick up a regular punter, even though it was her night off and she didn't need the money anymore. Debbie, true to her word, paid her for being a corner manager, and with the cash she made from prowling men, Lillibet had a decent income. No more worries about paying bills, hence why she'd been frivolous in Jackpot Palace.

People milled around, and she gazed through windows at those dining, wishing she'd had a stable life like they seemed to have. She'd dug her way out of her old life to get the one she had now. All right, she had to sell her body, but so what? She actually didn't mind it.

With no one she recognised taking the bait, she made up her mind to forgo a taxi and walk home. She only lived off the road at the end of the long strip that led from the Plaza. A tiny voice in her head told her to get a taxi anyway, like Debbie insisted—and because someone had been going round picking off working girls, raping and killing them, then leaving their bodies posed in weird positions.

A shiver went through her, so she took her phone out of her bag and called a cab. She liked living, so it was best she got herself home in one piece. She walked to the edge of the car park and waited beneath a streetlamp. A car coasted by, turned around, then came back. It stopped beside her, and the window went down about two inches. A pair of eyes appeared, the darkness in the interior disguising the rest of the features. Another shiver climbed up her spine, and she shook her head to say she wasn't available.

The car eased away, and she chanted the number plate while she put it in her work phone to send to Debbie. The twins could get their copper to put it through the database. Something about the driver had unnerved her, and she'd never forgive herself if she'd been this close to the killer and hadn't done anything about it. But was that only *because* there was a prostitute killer going around that she felt this way?

She put her phone in her bag and peered down the long, dark stretch of road with minimal lighting that led to her street. The car had parked, it's red taillights about halfway down, and she breathed a sigh of relief that her cab had turned up. As always, she took a picture of the taxi license and the plate, then got in the back.

"I'm just down there and round the corner," she said, giving her address.

"I can understand why you'd get a taxi for such a short walk," the driver said.

"Why, look like a prosser, do I?" She smiled so he knew she didn't mean any harm.

He met her eyes in the rearview mirror. "No, just that you're young and a woman. It's bloody nasty what's been going on this past month."

They drew close to the parked car. The window was still down those two inches, and as they passed, she caught a glint from the eyes reflected off the streetlight. She snapped her attention away and looked ahead, her heart rate picking up speed. She was just being daft, wasn't she, getting all het up? He was likely an old customer, otherwise, how would he have known what she did for a living to have approached her in the first place?

The cabbie parked outside her house, and she paid him, rushing inside and locking the door. She dashed into the living room and parted the curtains a little.

That car was outside, those eyes staring straight at her.

"Fuck," she whispered.

The driver got out, and no wonder she hadn't been able to make out his features. A balaclava covered his face. He walked up Lillibet's path and knocked on her door, the reverberation from it filtering into her body.

She fished her phone out to ring the police, hands shaking. The letterbox clattered, and she held her breath, thumb poised over the nine button on her keypad. The rumble of the engine filled Lillibet's ears, and she stared outside again, those red taillights straight ahead but in the distance.

She ran to the front door and picked up a folded piece of notepaper from the mat, waking her phone screen to use it as a torch. She opened the letter and stared down at the words, her body going cold, her legs weakening at the knees.

HELLO, LILLIBET. YOU'RE NEXT.

To be continued in *Ransack,*
The Cardigan Estate 25

Printed in Great Britain
by Amazon